BECAUSE OF MISS EVERDEAN

AMANDA MCCABE

Published by Oliver-Heber Books

0 9 8 7 6 5 4 3 2 1

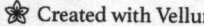

 Created with Vellum

To my very dear friends
Anne Wright Backus and Laura Kay Gauldin, for putting up with me for all these years.
What would I have done without you?

PROLOGUE

ENGLAND, 1814

HE WAS DEAD. REALLY, deeply, profoundly dead.

And she had killed him.

Lady Elizabeth Everdean nudged cautiously at the prone body of her affianced bridegroom with the toe of her slipper, moving one massive, flaccid arm all of two inches. He did not appear to be moving at all, and the stream of crimson that flowed from the back of his bald head was a very bad sign indeed.

Still, she wasn't absolutely certain. It seemed entirely impossible that someone who had caused such violence, such terror only an instant before should suddenly be so ... still. Choking back a terrified sob, she clutched her torn chemise around her naked breasts and knelt beside him.

Slowly, slowly she leaned forward, half afraid the closed eyes would suddenly fly open and the cold hands would reach for her again. She stretched out one finger and touched the pulse point on his wrinkled neck.

Nothing. Not a movement, not a breath. The ancient Duke of Leonard would never, could never, hurt her again. Not in this world. Elizabeth almost murmured a prayer of thanksgiving, before she realized that she was now in serious trouble.

She stumbled to her feet and fell back onto the rumpled bed, shaking with sobs. Right next to the murder weapon itself. With a small shriek, she shoved the bloodstained chamber pot onto the floor and buried her head in a pillow.

"Damn you to the furthest reaches of Hades, Peter!" she choked out, consigning her stepbrother to flames of torment with a furious swipe of her fist. "This is all your doing. Yours and mine."

She peered at the unmoving body of her "betrothed" through the tangled curtain of her black hair. And to think, when Peter had told her he had arranged a marriage for her she had been happy. Happy! As darkly comical as that seemed now, she had seen marriage as a way to leave Peter's household, a way to escape from the cold stranger he had become since his return from the Peninsula, a way to escape from their quarrels and icy silences—so different from the laughter of her childhood. She had dreamed of a handsome young gallant, who would take her to London where she could become the portrait painter to the ton, the Toast of the Town.

Ha! Had there ever been a more naive chit than she had been? Those dreams had died a hard death when she had come downstairs for their dinner party that very night and seen the duke waiting for her, ancient and portly and drooling. She would have run away right then and there, barricaded herself in her room, if Peter's iron grip on her satin-covered arm had not prevented her. She had had no choice but to bow her head and allow the duke to take her hand in his scaly palm.

She had thought she knew the worst life had to offer when she sat beside him at dinner, watching him down champagne and lobster patties as if they were nearing extinction. What very little she knew. What had happened after she retired, and the duke paid her a little "call," had been inestimably worse. It had been, in fact, like a painting she had once seen of the Last Judgment. Elizabeth now knew what those poor, doomed souls, flayed alive and shrieking, had felt when they were thrown to torment. Those snakelike hands had shoved her to the bed, the bed her mother and stepfather had once shared, and reached for her hem.

"You are mine now," he had panted in her face, his breath hot and reeking of garlic. "Your brother thinks he has the better of me, but he can think again, my pretty little whore." And he had latched his teeth onto her earlobe.

Elizabeth screamed then, screamed in mindless terror. Not even his slaps could silence her-she did not even feel them. As he turned to reach for a discarded petticoat to shove into her mouth, her desperate fingers had groped across the slippery sheets for something, anything, she could use in her own defense. She had only one thought now, desperate as a wounded animal, that she would surely die if this terrible assault went on.

Then she felt the cool, heavy porcelain of the chamber pot.

Thankfully, it was an empty chamber pot.

She had not meant to actually kill him. Just stop him from touching her.

Her own loud sobs, and a timid knocking at the door, jolted her into the present.

"Lady Elizabeth!" Daisy, Elizabeth's young maid,

pecked at the door again. "Was that you screaming, Lady Elizabeth?"

They knew! They knew what she had done, that she was a murderess, and now she would be dragged off and hanged, and Peter would laugh. All because of a pig like the duke. She was only eighteen—she did not want to die!

Life was so very unfair.

Daisy knocked at the door again, louder. "Lady Elizabeth, please! Is something amiss?"

They did not know! Of course they did not. Not at the moment, anyway. Taking a deep, steadying breath, she called, "I am quite all right, Daisy."

"Truly, my lady?" Daisy's voice was uncertain.

"Truly. I-I had a bad dream, that is all." Elizabeth shut her eyes tightly. If only that were true. "You may go. I will ring for you in the morning."

"Yes, my lady."

Elizabeth listened as Daisy's footsteps faded, then she ran across the room, tripping over her tattered hem, to where her armoire stood open. She scattered ball gowns, tea frocks, parasols, slippers, and bonnets onto the floor carelessly, pushing a change of clothes into a valise along with her mother's jewel case and a packet of letters from an old schoolfriend, the famous artist Georgina Beaumont. Georgie was in Italy now, far away from England, and she had always urged Elizabeth to join her.

Elizabeth felt that now would be an auspicious time to accept that offer.

On top of the clothes, she placed a carefully wrapped bundle of sketchbooks, pencils, and pigments.

"I have to leave," she whispered as she wriggled out of the ruined chemise. "There is no other way." As she turned to snatch up clean undergarments, she caught a glimpse of herself in the gilt-framed mirror above her dressing table. Purple bruises darkened her pale shoulders and small breasts; blood had caked at the corner of her mouth. She was suddenly disgusted, nauseous, at such vivid proof of what had happened this horrible night. She grabbed up the lethal chamber pot and deposited the meager contents of her stomach.

When the illness had passed, Elizabeth knelt there on the floor, naked and trembling, unable to cry or think or do anything.

She swore, then and there, that no man would have such power over her again. Her father, her step-father, her brother, the duke—all the men in her life had caused her naught but sorrow. From then on, she would not be Lady Elizabeth, pampered daughter and helpless pawn. She was simply Elizabeth, and she would be fine on her own.

1

LONDON, TWO YEARS LATER

"BY THE GODS, IT IS Old Nick."

Nicholas Hollingsworth, now Sir Nicholas Hollingsworth, late of His Majesty's Army and with a knighthood for valor on the battlefield, raised his dark gaze from the cards in his hand. He squinted through the haze of cigar smoke and brandy fumes until he met a pair of cold blue eyes he had never thought to see again this side of Hell.

"Peter Everdean." His voice was steady, low, despite the turmoil in his brain, in his soul. "Is it you? Alive?"

"Sorry are you, Nick?" The golden-haired man smiled sweetly, Mephisto disguised as Gabriel.

Around them, the tumult of the gaming hell went on, men laughing and shouting, bottles shattering, smoke billowing, fortunes won and lost, lives changing on the turn of a card. But to Nicholas, as he folded the cards carefully in his long fingers and laid them on the table, none of the London decadence existed any longer.

He was back on a scorching Spanish battlefield, and the smoke was now cannon fire, the smell acrid in his nostrils, the dirt under his worn boots slippery with blood. He felt again the sharp pain in his leg, the wet, sticky warmth of his own blood, the numb sensation of falling, falling.

A pair of blue eyes above him, a voice telling him they would soon reach the field hospital, not letting him fall any further. Not letting him die. Nicholas shook his head fiercely. He rose to his feet, perfectly steady despite the quantity of brandy he had consumed that night, his knuckles white on the silver head of his walking stick. He moved carefully toward the elegant figure who waited in the smoke, not entirely sure he wasn't more drunk than he had thought. Or dreaming.

"I thought you were dead," he breathed.

"Certainly not." Peter's voice was as cool, as controlled as ever. "I am far too wicked to die. As, I see, are you, Old Nick." He gestured toward Nicholas with his quizzing glass, taking in the long scar on his tanned cheek, the walking stick that was more than a mere fashionable accessory.

"Quite. Just a bit the worse for wear." Nicholas ran his hand through his thick black curls, uncharacteristically bemused. Here he was, standing in a noisy London hell, conversing calmly with the "late" Peter Everdean, as if four long years had been nothing. Peter was still the golden Apollo to Nick's Hephaestus—slender, charming, graceful, still able to gain every girl's eye, be she duchess or Spanish peasant.

And still as cold as a witch's. Hmm.

Nicholas had seen the truth of Peter long ago, when they had lodged together in Spain. Peter was a man with some secret torment, some demon that rode him. He was charming, yes, an excellent companion, but unpredictable.

Entirely the wrong companion for wild Old Nick

Hollingsworth, bastard son of the Earl of Ainsley, whose father had bought him a commission in the hopes he would stick his spoon in the wall in Spain, and cause the Ainsleys no more trouble with his escapades. Together, Nick and Peter had been the terrors of the Army.

And Peter had saved his life, practically carried him miles to a field hospital. Then disappeared. A physician had told Nicholas, when he awoke from his delirium, that his rescuer had died later that day. Now here he was, alive, whole, the same Peter.

With the same flashing, secret torment in his eyes. And Nick owed him so very much. Owed him his very life.

Now Peter smiled at him coolly, swinging the quizzing glass by its long ribbon. "You know, my friend," he said. "You may be just the man who can help me."

A SHORT CARRIAGE RIDE LATER, Peter sat down behind his massive library desk and waved Nick to a nearby armchair. "I have been living rather quietly in the country since the war, gotten involved with local politics, that sort of thing." He held out a box of expensive cigars, waiting for Nicholas to take one before he chose for himself. "But I am not altogether isolated in Derbyshire. I've heard of you."

"Indeed?" Nicholas grinned.

"Indeed, Old Nick. I read the scandal sheets."

"Doesn't seem your sort of reading material, Everdean. Or should I say, Clifton." Nicholas leaned back in his chair, enjoying the cigar, the familiarity of Peter's cynical company.

"Someone at Clifton Manor enjoys them greatly. I merely read them when they happen to be lying about, of course."

"Of course," Nicholas replied, all innocence.

"Yes. Your name is always there. Duels, brawls, hearts broken, horse races won. They say you refused to marry the Woodley chit when you danced with her three times at Almack's."

"I only danced with her once, and of course I would never marry her. She has less conversation than my horse, and is not nearly as pretty."

"Ha! And what was the latest? That opera dancer? Celine Lacroix?"

Nicholas laughed out loud, more at Peter's coolly raised brow than at the memory of the fiery mademoiselle. "She stood in front of my house screaming and throwing rocks at the windows. Woke the whole neighborhood, not to mention that she broke five windows."

"You had given the lady her *congé*. Quite understandable that she would be upset." Peter clicked his tongue in mock sympathy. "But really, Nick, you cannot devote your life to tormenting your father's family forever, you know."

Nicholas sighed. "I know, I know. But since the war, there is not much need for the meager skills I possess."

Peter studied him for a long moment. "What have you been doing, besides drinking and whoring?"

Nicholas looked down at the smoldering tip of his

cigar. "Forgetting, of course. As I am sure you are. And having a very good time in the process."

"Old Nick, eh?"

"Quite."

"If you ever happen to become bored with that, I have a task that might amuse you."

Nicholas sat up straight, his interest caught by something in Peter's voice, a distant longing perhaps, a hint of steel. "Do tell."

"Perhaps you will recall, two years ago my household was involved in some unpleasantness, which I do not like to recall."

Nicholas frowned. "Yes, of course, Clifton. I did not connect it to you. I was in Paris at the time."

Yet the tale had reached even to Paris. The Earl of Clifton's sister, fleeing her home the night of her betrothal, leaving behind a very elderly, very dead fiancé. Clifton had put it about that the deceased duke had died of a heart attack, hinted that it had come about because of his exertions in the bed of a housemaid, and that his sister had retreated in heartbreak to distant relatives.

Not that anyone actually believed that. But the Earl of Clifton was rumored to be as ruthless as he was reclusive, and the heirs to the dead duke had been hardly prostrate with grief, but rather elated to inherit the title and estates. The scandal had soon died down, and there had been no inquiry.

Peter's eyes flashed a blue fire, quickly hidden by golden lashes. "I need someone, someone I can trust, to find my sister and bring her back to England."

Nicholas almost fell out of his chair. Him, as the finder of lost brides, the seeker of runaway debutantes? Ludicrous. Absurd. "I understood the young lady to be in Cornwall. Or was it Devon?"

Peter's pale hands tightened. "Neither. I've recently received word she may be in Italy."

"And you want me to find her?" Nicholas rose to his feet, convinced completely that his old friend had truly gone mad at last. "Italy is a very large place, Everdean, and there are many locations where a runaway heiress could hide."

"There is no place where she could hide from Nicholas Hollingsworth, surely. It is very important that Elizabeth be brought back here to me. Soon. And there is no one I trust to do it, as I trust you. Remember Spain? We are old friends. Are we not?"

Nicholas looked into those ice blue eyes, and saw there all he owed Peter Everdean. His life might be worthless, wasted in drink and women, but he liked living it all the same. If it had not been for Peter, he would be lying even now in a mass grave in Spain.

Perhaps a sojourn in Italy would do him some good.

He slowly sat back down "I don't even know what your sister looks like."

A small smile never reached Peter's eyes. "That is easily rectified. And Elizabeth is actually my stepsister. Her mother married my father."

Peter pushed a small inlaid box across the desk. Nicholas lifted the lid, and there was the most lovely woman he had ever seen in his thirty-four years. And he had seen some.

No, he amended, as he studied the miniature portrait closer. She was not beautiful. Her sweet, heart-shaped face and narrow shoulders above a purple satin bodice almost gave her the appearance of a child. Her slender neck seemed to bend with the weight of black hair, swept up and entwined with pearls and amethysts. Yet her wide, blue-gray eyes seemed to speak to him in some way. The curve of her shell-pink lips indicated some wonderful, precious secret that she would divulge only to him.

She was a woodland fairy, dark and enticing and elusive as the mist.

Nicholas looked up to find Peter watching him. He closed the box with a loud snap. A beautiful sprite Elizabeth Everdean might be, but Nick owed Peter a great debt. And rogue though he was, Nicholas always paid his debts. "Where is she now?"

Peter smiled again, a rare genuine smile of what? Relief? Gratitude? Expectation? Whatever, it was gone in an instant. He reached into a drawer and withdrew a slim letter. "A friend who was traveling in Venice says she saw a girl answering to Elizabeth's description in the San Giacometto."

"Venice?" The old soldier in Nick had taken over, pushing aside the indolent roué. His muscles tensed, his mind raced, hungry for the chase again. He sat forward in his chair. "This friend is reliable?"

"Quite. And Elizabeth is very distinctive. She may be dark, like the Italians, but there cannot be two ladies like her in all of Europe." Peter took up the inlaid box and opened it, smiling down at the painted image. "There cannot. And Italy is just where she would have fled. Elizabeth fancies herself an artist, and indeed she is quite good."

Nicholas felt a frisson of unease ripple down his spine as he watched his old friend trace a pale, long finger over the painted dark hair. Shaking his head, he pushed the unease away. "Venice is not so large a place. It should not take very long."

Peter glanced up sharply. "'Then you will do it? You will find Elizabeth?"

"I will. For you."

Peter nodded and looked back down at the painted girl. "Then your debt will be paid."

2

VENICE

"THERE HE IS AGAIN!" Elizabeth hissed urgently at Georgina from behind her fan, barely audible over the raucous music and the laughter of the dancers. The Contessa de Torre's famous masked ball, held every year to begin Carnivale, was famously wild, and this year was no exception. Napoleon was gone, Italy was free (perhaps a bit too free), and the Venetians were in the mood for merrymaking.

And Elizabeth had been having an absolutely splendid time, imbibing the excellent champagne and dancing with her quite attractive, if rather somber, sometime-suitor, the sculptor Sir Stephen Hampton. She had laughed and flirted and cavorted, and had been enjoying lingering at supper with a crowd of fellow artists.

Until she had seen him.

He had been in the Piazza San Marco that morning, she was certain of it. Watching her as she sketched. Then, when she had made up her mind to confront him, he had been gone.

Like mist.

She had been suspicious, yes. After all, it had been rather too quiet on the Peter front for over two years, and she had not expected him to simply let her go as easily as he had. But, more than suspecting the man's motives for watching her, she had wanted to paint him. So much so that she had ached with a need to put his features down on canvas.

In her travels with Georgina, Elizabeth had seen many men. Wealthy men, handsome men, well-dressed and witty men, some of whom had shown a more-than-polite interest in her. A few of the models she had seen in artists' studios had been almost god-like in their physical beauty. Her own stepbrother, as annoying as he was, was a veritable Apollo.

But she had never, ever seen a man like this one. When he had vanished before she could so much as trace a rough outline of him, she had almost thrown a tantrum right in the middle of the crowded piazza. Well, he was not going anywhere now. Elizabeth left off trying to gain Georgina's attention, and forgetting the revels of the night, forgetting even basic good manners, she propped her elbow on the table, rested her chin in her palm, and stared.

He was tall, taller than almost any man there, and much taller than her own diminutive five feet. Despite the fact that it was supposed to be *un hallo in maschera*, he wore modern evening dress, stark black and white, impeccably tailored over his wide shoulders. ıhe only flash of color was a small ruby in his simply tied cravat. His hair was unfashionably long, as black as her own, but curling where hers was stick straight.

Not even a white, jagged, wicked-looking scar slicing across his cheek could detract from his powerful, primitive, masculine beauty.

How she would love to paint him. As the god Hades in his underworld. In a little toga. Or maybe even nothing.

He was just altogether perfect. As beautifully made as the marble statues she had seen in Rome and Florence. Except that those were cold, white marble, and this man was obviously warm, golden flesh. Yet, despite her appreciation for his wide shoulders, it was his eyes that really caught her, that made her completely unable to look away from him. They were the deepest, darkest brown she had ever seen, almost black, and it was like falling into soft velvet to look into them. Warm velvet, that invited confidences, coaxed secrets from a woman's heart, but gave up none in return.

She, who had learned to be adept at reading people through their faces, their expressions, their eyes, could tell absolutely nothing about this man. He revealed nothing at all.

Oh, not even dear Stephen, who had escorted her dutifully about Venice, could come close to this man! Elizabeth flashed an apologetic glance at the redheaded sculptor who sat beside her, then looked back to the dark stranger.

Only to find him staring right back at her.

Elizabeth gasped, and dropped her gaze back to her lap in bewilderment. Then she peeked up.

Her eyes dropped again. He was laughing at her! "Fool, fool!" she whispered, pounding her forehead with the palm of her hand. "Gaping like the veriest lackwit."

"Did you say something, Lizzie?" Georgina turned to Elizabeth at last, her cheeks still pomegranate red from the lively debate she had been leading on the merits of oils over tempera.

"Not a thing." Elizabeth snapped open her fan, waving it so vigorously that tendrils of black hair escaped from the gilded netting that held the heavy mass in place.

"Oh. I thought you were just agreeing with me about what a fool Ottavio is!"

This released a flood of Italian invective from the slighted Ottavio. Georgina laughed merrily, tossed her gorgeous auburn head, and looked back to Elizabeth.

Her eyes traced to where Elizabeth was peeking, and widened.

"Ahhh," she breathed. "I see."

"See what?" Elizabeth dared another look. The object of her admiration was deep in conversation with their hostess. The contessa, every buxom inch of her almost exposed in her silver satin Cleopatra costume, was pressed against his arm, laughing up into his eyes.

One of the sticks of Elizabeth's abused fan snapped in her fingers.

Georgina smiled. "I see, Lizzie, that that is just the sort of man you need."

"What!" Elizabeth gasped. She had traveled with Georgina for two years, had heard every imaginable risqué remark issue from her friend's crimson lips, but she was still moved to blush at times. "Why, whatever do you mean?"

"That man there. The one you are ogling as if he were a particularly delectable cream puff in Seganti's bakery window." Georgina pointed with the jeweled dagger of her lady-pirate costume, waving the sharp tip around erratically until Elizabeth grasped her wrist and forced her to cease. "He is just what you need."

Elizabeth blinked in confusion. Had Georgina, always a bit eccentric, slipped into complete madness and begun to procure men to satisfy Elizabeth's "lusts"?

"Need for what, Georgie?"

"For your secretary, of course! Your man-of-affairs, your aide-de-camp. Don't you remember our conversation yesterday? What did you think I meant?" Georgina's brows rose. "Oh. Oh! Never say you, our little nun, were thinking of other affairs besides accounts payable when you saw this dark mystery man!"

Their small circle guffawed loudly, drunkenly, banter flying as Elizabeth felt herself slowly turning crimson.

"How the mighty have fallen!" Georgina said. "The nun is in lust!"

Elizabeth groaned, and buried her face in her hands.

"Really, Georgina!" Sir Stephen sniffed. "Must you always be so crude?"

"Really, Stevie!" Georgina mimicked. "Must you be such a prig? We're only teasing Elizabeth a little. A very little."

"Stop it!" Elizabeth cut off her friends' familiar squabbling with a wave of her hand, and managed to lift her champagne glass for a comforting swallow. She only wished it were something a bit stronger.

Georgina slid her gold brocade-clad arm around Elizabeth's shoulders. "I am sorry I embarrassed you, Lizzie, but do admit it. You did feel something, er, less than pure when you looked at that handsome bit of manhood."

Elizabeth blushed anew. "I really, no, I thought no such thing. I merely thought I should, well, paint him."

Liar, her conscience screamed. Paint him in honey, mayhap, and lick him from chin to toe.

No! Elizabeth fanned herself with the mangled fan

again, trying desperately to appear unaffected and unconcerned.

"Oh, Lizzie, dear, of course you want him! And who could blame you," Georgina whispered. "So handsome. And that wicked scar. Very piratical."

Elizabeth gave in to Georgina's gentle teasing with a giggle. "Shall he make me swab the deck, do you think?"

"Only if you are very fortunate. Or walk the plank?"

Elizabeth laughed outright at that, leaning helplessly against Georgina's shoulder. "That does sound intriguing!"

"What exactly is the plank, Lizzie?"

"Why, whatever I want it to be, of course!" Elizabeth blithely reached for a nearby champagne bottle and poured the last of it into her empty glass.

Georgina nodded approvingly. "It is time you showed such an interest, my cloistered friend." She speared a chunk of roast duckling with her dagger and popped it into her mouth, chewing thoughtfully. "I had begun to despair of you, Lizzie, especially when you turned that heavenly Marchese Luddovicco in Rome down flat." She pointed the dagger at an oblivious Sir Stephen. "I had thought Monsieur Sculptor over there would be as lusty as you were going to get!"

"Georgie! Stephen and I are merely friends, as you well know."

"And I know he would like to be more! He is all wrong for you, Lizzie."

Elizabeth felt it best to turn the topic. "You are one to talk, Georgie! I have not seen you 'take such an interest' since that model in Milan. What was his name? Paolo?"

Georgina speared another piece of duckling. "Bah!

Men. Who needs them?" She seemed totally unaware of the irony of this. "I had two worthless husbands in five years—worthless but for their money, that is, and Paolo was becoming far too bossy. For all his gorgeous dark eyes, I felt it was kinder to remove myself from the situation. Why did you think we left Milan in such a hurry?"

Elizabeth giggled into her champagne.

"But you, Lizzie," Georgina continued. "You need to have some fun. You are so young, and you act like such an old matron sometimes. I would wager that handsome rogue over there is just what you re- quire. For the present, anyway."·

Elizabeth rolled her eyes. "There is no talking sense to you tonight, Georgina Beaumont! So I am going out onto the terrace for some fresh air."

"Shall I accompany you, Elizabeth?" Stephen rose to his feet, rather awkward in his Caesar costume. He kept attempting to pull the toga down to cover his knees, and his laurel wreath was askew over his brow.

Georgina reached over, grabbed a handful of that toga, and pulled him back down into his chair. "Of *course* she does not need you to accompany her, nodcock!" She totally ignored his icy glare, and waved her fingers at Elizabeth's retreating figure. "She is going outside completely alone, I am sure. That is the best way to, ahem, take the air."

Elizabeth, feeling very childish, stuck out her tongue at her laughing friends. Then she turned, swept out onto the terrace and immediately tripped over the boots of the dark stallion.

It was her.

When Nicholas had first seen the woman, garbed as Juliet in forest-green velvet and gold lace, laughing and talking, he had known. Just as he had known that morning, when he saw her sketching a group of giggling Italian children in the Piazza San Marco, a beribboned straw hat half-hiding her face.

He had found Lady Elizabeth Everdean. And she was not precisely what he had been expecting.

Oh, she was pretty, just as her portrait had promised, small and delicate, pale and midnight dark. He had been told she was interested in art, but he had never expected to find her actually making her fortune in the medium, much less surrounded by a racy crowd of champagne-flushed artists.

When her partner, a tall, patrician-looking man dressed as a Roman with wreath and toga, had put his hand on her arm with obvious familiarity, Nicholas's fingers had reached convulsively for the pistol hidden in his velvet jacket.

For one shattering instant he had forgotten the debt he owed Peter Everdean. He had forgotten everything, and only seen this Elizabeth as a woman.

A lovely woman he wanted for himself.

He wanted to feel her small, pale body naked against his, to breathe in her scent, to ease into her welcoming warmth, and hear her sigh and cry out his name

He needed some air.

Nicholas evaded the clinging arms of his hostess, and retreated in haste to the darkness of the terrace, to breathe in the quiet, the solitude.

He was not to be solitary very long.

No sooner had he lit a thin cigar and leaned back to enjoy it, than a bundle of green velvet and lilies-of-the-valley scent tumbled through the doors and landed at his feet.

"H-hello," the bundle whispered.

Nicholas found himself gaping like the veriest green lad at the lady's stocking-clad calves and slim ankles above high-heeled green satin shoes. He blinked and quickly raised his eyes to her face. She was half in shadow, yet he could still see the flush across her high cheekbones, and the way she was, in tum, gaping up at him.

"Signorina," he murmured, automatically making a polite leg. "Or is it signora?"

"It-it is signorina," she answered, still whispering.

Nicholas's smile was white and predatory in the darkness as he looked down at her. At last. Signorina Everdean.

3

Elizabeth silently willed the marble beneath her bottom to open up and swallow her whole. When it chose not to oblige, and instead left her sprawled inelegantly at the feet of the most attractive man she had ever encountered, she slowly opened her eyes and dared a peek up at him.

"Good evening!" she chirped, then closed her eyes again when she heard how mortifyingly high-pitched her voice had suddenly become. Coughing as delicately as possible, she tried again. "Delightful party, is it not?"

"Delightful," the man answered, his voice warm and rough, dark as the night around them. Indeed, he seemed almost a part of the night, his black hair and attire blending into the midnight darkness, leaving only the glow of his eyes as he looked down at her, unsmiling.

Elizabeth resisted the urge to titter, something she had not been at all tempted to do since she left the schoolroom. Instead, she leaned back and said coolly, "I do not believe I have ever seen you in Venice before, signor."

"No. I have only just arrived."

A man of few words. Excellent. Then Elizabeth's eyes widened, as she registered that the man's words had been in perfectly unaccented English. "You are English!"

"Indeed I am."

"I thought I knew all the English who were staying here." She ran through all her acquaintances in her mind, but all of them, even the most eccentric poets and painters, seemed far too, well, *ordinary* to be associated with this man. And no one had mentioned they were expecting a new houseguest. "But then, we have only been here three months ourselves, though Venice is so wonderful it feels only days! We were in Milan before. Have you been to Milan?"

"No."

"You ought to go. It is quite fascinating. I learned a great deal there. In fact, I did not want to leave, but Georgie—Georgina—insisted we come here for Carnivale."

Elizabeth almost slapped herself. She was babbling. She, who could fend off every overbold swain with a sharp word and a snap of her fingers! She, whom a disappointed suitor had once dubbed the Ice Duchess. She was rattling on like a sapskull, all because a handsome man was looking down at her in the moonlight. She snapped her mouth shut and fell silent.

He held out one hand to help her to her feet, quite startling Elizabeth since she had forgotten she was sprawled out on the cold marble with her skirts about her knees. She reached up tentatively and took the proffered hand; his slightly callused palm felt warm and cool against her skin. She did not want to let go, even when she was firmly on her feet again. And he seemed quite willing to let her go on holding his hand.

"Where were you, before you were in Milan?" he asked softly, so close that his breath stirred the loose curls at her temples.

"What?" she murmured absently, quite absorbed in the smell of him, evergreen and starch and something darker, richer. She wanted to bury her nose in his satin waistcoat and inhale him.

"I said where did you live, before you were in Milan? In a rose petal?"

"A what?"

"A rose petal. Is that not where all fairy princesses curl up to sleep?" His aged-cognac voice was lightly amused, as if she were a diverting child he was attempting to humor.

A child was the very last thing she wanted to be in this man's eyes. Fairy princess, however, sounded slightly more promising. "I don't know about fairies, signor, but I sleep in an ordinary feather bed."

"Indeed? And I thought I had found an escapee from fairyland, with eyes the color of the stormy sea."

Elizabeth giggled despite herself. She looked down, turning his hand between both of hers, and imagined raising the bronze flesh to her lips, pressing kisses along the callused ridge of the heel of his palm, where he would grip a sword. Suddenly lightheaded, she dropped his hand and stepped back, forcing herself to take in deep breaths of the cool night air.

But her lungs were still filled with the scent of him.

It was just the champagne, clouding her very judgment, making her behave foolishly. That was all. She was only tipsy. Really.

"We lived in Rome," she answered finally, turning her back on his disturbing presence to look down over the Grand Canal and the gondolas filled with revelers that floated there. One couple, cloaked and masked, waved up at her and she waved back. "In rented rooms, remarkably free of any resemblance to a rose petal. Before that we were at the small villa Georgie owns, at Lake Como."

"We?" He had moved silently closer, and she could feel his warmth against her velvet-covered back.

"My sister and myself. We are artists, and must travel to find patrons."

"Women artists?"

Elizabeth stiffened, bracing for the inevitable mockery. Please, not him, too. Yet there was only curiosity in his voice, and an odd sort of tension, waiting. "Yes," she answered. "Georgina, my sister, is becoming quite well known. In England she painted Mrs. Drummond-Burrell's portrait. Perhaps you have heard of her? Mrs. Georgina Beaumont?"

"I have indeed." He leaned against the marble balustrade behind him, his velvet sleeve brushing lightly against her hand. "She was quite the *on dit* in London. Even from afar she excites much interest."

Elizabeth couldn't help but laugh. "Every bit of it true, I assure you! Georgie causes a stir wherever we go."

"I was not aware she had a sister who is also an artist."

"Oh, I am still a student, really. I am, however, working on a new commission at the moment."

"Indeed?"

"Yes. A portrait of Katerina Bruni." She glanced at him from the comer of her eye, gauging his reaction to the name of the infamous, and very beautiful, courtesan. "Another scandalous lady, *n'est-ce pas*?"

He laughed, the rich sound of it flowing through her like creamy chocolate. "The mistress of the Marquis of Rothmere is well known everywhere, yes. She is a famous beauty, and notoriously particular about who paints her portrait. You are doing very well for a mere student."

Elizabeth shrugged, secretly pleased at the compliment. "The Italians are very friendly, and quite receptive to new artists. Much more so than the English." As the moon appeared from behind a bank of clouds, she turned back to her companion, to study his beautiful, scarred face. "That does not, however, mean they are any more prompt in paying their debts. And my name is Elizabeth Cheswood. It was quite rag-mannered of me not to introduce myself earlier."

"I am very pleased to meet you, Miss Cheswood."

Elizabeth waited expectantly, but no reciprocal information was forthcoming. "You have not told me your name, signor, or where you were before you came to Venice."

He shrugged, the dark cloth of his coat rippling impressively across his back and shoulders. "I am not at all interesting, Miss Cheswood. I fear I would bore you with the mundane details of my life."

"I am not bored yet," she answered quietly.

A muscle clenched in his smooth-sculpted jaw. "My name is Nicholas, and I was in London before I came to Venice and found you." He smiled at her tightly. "There—you see, Miss Cheswood? Quite ordinary."

"Oh, I hardly think you could be called ordinary, Nicholas of London." The champagne seemed to be making her bold. She traced the jagged scar on his cheek lightly with her fingertip, and, though his entire body was tense as a cracked whip, he did not move away. "Quite the opposite, I would say."

"Oh, yes?" His voice was hardly more than a rough

whisper, and he reached out to lightly caress her cheek.

"Yes." Elizabeth hardly knew what she was doing. She had never in her life been so very close to a man, a stranger. But she went on tiptoe, her palm flat against his cheek now, their breath mingling. His arm crept about her waist. "Have you ever had your portrait painted, Nicholas?"

"Never. Should you like to be the first to paint it?" His mouth almost, barely, delicately touched hers. Her eyes drifted shut.

"Elizabeth! What are you doing out here?"

"Blast!" she breathed, jerking out of Nicholas's embrace and turning to glare at the interloper. "Stephen."

"Elizabeth!" Stephen said sternly, waving his shield at her. "Your sister wishes to speak with you, and she feels you have been out in this cold air long enough."

"Georgie sent you?" Elizabeth fumed, her tiny fists planted on her hips. "I hardly think that is the situation! What do you—"

Her words ended in an indignant squeak, as Stephen seized her arm in a surprisingly strong grasp and marched her from the terrace. Her feet did not even touch the floor as he swept her back inside the doors and into the midst of the noisy, overheated party.

She only managed one frantic glance over her shoulder at the shadowy figure, who blew her an impertinent kiss.

She did not see Georgina lurking behind a potted plant, twisting her brocade sleeve thoughtfully as she watched the man who, shaking only slightly, was lighting a thin cigar and turning to watch the canal again.

"Signor!" she called, rustling forward. "Signor, we

have not been formally introduced, but my name is Mrs. Georgina Beaumont. I could not help but notice that you were just in earnest conversation with my sister"

"Ah. So you are the famous Mrs. Beaumont?"

"I am. And you are?"

"Nicholas Carter." He made an elegant leg. "At your service."

Georgina flashed a roguish smile. "I do hope so, sirrah. Or rather, that you are at my sister's service."

"I am afraid I do not understand."

"Would you perhaps be in need of employment, Mr. Carter? While you are in fair Venice? Something I think you would find amusing."

His dark eyes flashed down at her. "Just what are you suggesting, Mrs. Beaumont?"

4

"Bianca! How can I draw if you persist in wriggling about so?" Elizabeth snapped. "You swore you would remain still this time."

The little Italian maid, garbed in classical draperies formed of sheets and a braided curtain cord, twisted about again, pouting extravagantly. "But, signorina! Someone is knocking at your door, and it is my duty to answer it! I am maid."

"Your predominant duty at the moment is to be my model," Elizabeth muttered. As she lowered the drawing pencil clutched in her fingers, she finally heard Georgina pounding on the bedroom door.

Georgie sounded far too cheerful by half, considering it was not even noon yet.

"Yoo-hoo! Lizzie!" she sang, beating a pattern on the door. "Are you there, dear?"

"Come in, if you must," Elizabeth answered, bending back over her sketchbook. She had spent a sleepless night, going over and over in her mind the encounter with the dark Englishman, coming up with witty repartee she should have made instead of the nonsense she had spouted. As a result, she was bleary-eyed and cranky, with no patience for Georgina's shining good cheer.

"Oh, Lizzie." Georgina tsked, peeking around the door with bright eyes and perfectly coiffed auburn curls. "You are still in your night rail! And here it is almost time for luncheon."

"I am busy. And are you not supposed to be working?" Elizabeth pushed a tangle of black hair out of her eyes and watched, disgruntled, as Georgina bustled about, opening the armoire and searching through the jumble of Elizabeth's gowns.

"Indeed I do have work to do, a sitting with that tiresome old contessa and her nasty poodle. But right now I have a much more amusing task!"

Georgina was fairly vibrating with the need to tell something, so Elizabeth gave in with a sigh, and set aside her sketchbook. "Very well, what is it?"

"You have a caller."

"What? Who? At this time of day? If it is Stephen, you can tell him to go away. I am still angry with him over his high-handed behavior last night. We are not engaged, and the fact that—"

Georgina sniffed deprecatingly. "No, it is not that fussy old Stephen! I do not know why you bother with him at all, Lizzie. He is a talented sculptor, I admit, but he is so very *English*! We came to Italy to get away from that, did we not? There are so many attractive men in Venice. You could do ever so much better."

Elizabeth rattled her sketchbook impatiently at this oft-repeated refrain. "Enough, Georgie! I already know your opinion of poor Stephen. He and I are merely friends, in any case. So, if he is not downstairs, who is?" Her lips thinned. "Not a bill collector!"

Georgina paused to examine herself in the full-length looking glass, and straightened the green spencer that matched her green-and-gold striped walking dress. She was too obviously enjoying Elizabeth's impatience. "For once, Lizzie, it is not. You ought to pay more attention when those past-due notices arrive, dear. And you know I will lend you anything you need."

"I have more important things to worry about than bills, and you know I cannot take any more of your money." Elizabeth waved her pencil significantly. "And there is this sketch I am working on."

"Oh, I know you have better things to do than bother with ledger books and bills and contracts. And this caller is the very one to solve your problems."

Elizabeth frowned suspiciously. "Yes?"

"Yes. It is someone come to inquire about the position of your secretary."

"I told you, Georgie, I have no need of a secretary! We do well on our own, do we not? This hiring of an extra man was all your idea. And I could hardly pay another set of wages, could I? Not since my advance from Signora Bruni is almost gone, and Bianca costs so much."

The maid rustled her draperies in a great show of Italian indignation. "I am not just maid, signorina, I am model! Is very hard work."

Georgina merely smiled the smugly secretive smile that had been infuriating Elizabeth since their long-ago days at Miss Thompson's School for Young Ladies, when Elizabeth had idolized the sophisticated older girl. "Oh, believe me, Lizzie, you will want to meet with this person."

Elizabeth froze. No. It could not be. Could it?

"It is the dark lord from the ball last night!" Georgina crowed dramatically.

Elizabeth let out a tiny squeak. Her pencil fell

from numb fingers, scattering parchment every which way. "Nicholas," she whispered.

Georgina clapped her hands, dancing around the room on her small green half-boots. "Is it not wonderful, marvelous?"

"Buthow?"

Georgina suddenly whirled to a stop, and looked innocently down at her fingernails. "Fate, Lizzie. It was meant to be."

Elizabeth clicked her tongue knowingly. "Um-hm. Fate. A redheaded fate."

"Oh, Lizzie, don't fuss! What does it matter how he came here? It was obviously meant to be." Her eyes narrowed. "It is just such a pity you look as if you had been dragged through a cow pasture, dear. You are not a charwoman, you know."

Elizabeth's gaze flew to the mirror. She did indeed look like the proverbial beggar girl. Her hair straggled from its loose plait, falling over her face and her nightgown-clad shoulders like limp black linguini, and her face was chalky and hollow from lack of sleep and a surfeit of champagne. She dragged the nightgown over her head, and fled to her dressing room clad only in a silky chemise.

"Fear not, Cinderella!" Georgina sang, producing a comb from her pocket. "Your fairy godmother is here."

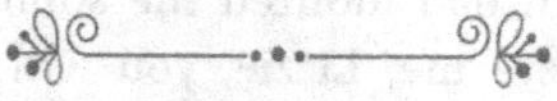

THE ELIZABETH who finally emerged from her room was completely unrecognizable as the shrieking raga-muffin she had been not fifteen minutes before. Her hair was neatly plaited and coiled in a gleaming coronet atop her head, fastened with ivory combs. She was freshly attired in a blue sprigged muslin morning gown, and she smelled of her favorite lilies-of-the-valley perfume. Bianca and Georgina waved her off like proud mamas at a night at Almack's.

And if she was tugging on stockings and slippers as she hopped one-legged down the stairs, who was to notice?

She paused at the foot of the stairs, half hidden by the newel post as she peered through the open door of their small drawing room. It was Nicholas. The dark man who had almost kissed her in the moonlight, and who had haunted her night. She had almost come to the conclusion that he had only been a dream, an enchantment of the night. Night in Venice could be quite intoxicating, after all; it could make things, and people, who were really quite ordinary seem almost earth-shattering.

Now she saw she had been quite wrong to suppose he could ever be ordinary in any light. He was impossibly, piratically elegant amid the comfortable shabbiness of their rented furniture. Today, his unfashionably long hair was held back in a neat, black-ribbon-tied queue, revealing the clean, strong line of his throat and jaw as he tilted back his head to look at a painting on the wall. His blue coat and buff breeches fit him like a second skin; his boots were glossy with a champagne polish.

And she felt like the lowliest beggar girl, despite Bianca and Georgina's efforts. She longed to run back and out in her violet silk, her best day dress. But he had already turned, and seen her lurking there, watching him.

With a deep breath, Elizabeth pasted on her brightest smile and stepped forward, hand outstretched. She just hoped he would not notice the smudges of charcoal across her knuckles, or the paint beneath her nails. "Mr. Nicholas! Such a surprise."

He lifted her proffered fingers to his lips, his breath warm and sweet on her skin. "I had heard that you were in need of a secretary, Miss Cheswood."

Secretary? What could that be? Every thought had flown out of her head at the sound of his voice. "Where could you have heard that?" she answered, surprised that her voice sounded so steady and normal when her heart was bursting.

"Shall we say, a small bird told me? A small red bird."

She could not help but laugh at the wicked glint in his dark eyes. "Oh, I see. Yes." She seated herself as regally as possible on a threadbare chaise, attempting to tuck her feet beneath her so that he could not see that her stocking had slipped from its garter and fallen to her ankle. Kicking off her slipper, she tried to pull the tube of silk up with the toes of her opposite foot.

"You did not mention that you were in need of a position," she said. She gestured to the fine cut of his clothes, the unscuffed boots. "Indeed, you do not look as if you need to work at all."

"Appearances can be deceiving, Miss Cheswood. You would do well to remember that." Nicholas turned back to the painting he had been studying when she came in. "Is this your work?"

Elizabeth's mouth softened as she examined the painting, a portrait of a young mother and her infant. "Yes. The woman was a peasant, who brought us fresh milk and eggs when we were at Lake Como. She was beautiful, like a Madonna. It is one of my favorites, but it is an early work of mine, very rough."

Nicholas tilted his head, taking in the smiling, golden-haired mother and her fat *bambino*. The lines were rather rough, the background of rolling hills and trees clumsily drawn, but the woman's vibrant personality shone like a fine red wine on a summer day. The vivid blue of her skirt shimmered. It was obvious that Elizabeth saw people, saw their true essence, and captured that on canvas. It was remarkable.

Then his gaze shifted from the smiling peasant woman to another mother, painted on a smaller canvas. This mother was pale, her red-gold hair falling over silk-covered shoulders, her blue-gray eyes smiling at the toddler beside her. There was something about those eyes. "She looks remarkably like you," he blurted out.

"She should. She was my mother." Elizabeth ran her eyes over the woman's painted green gown, the fall of her hair. "She died when I was nine, long before I ever picked up a paintbrush. This was from memory. It was—I don't know. Fantasy? I simply—" Then she came back to herself, to the dark eyes intent on her, and she could have bitten her tongue for running on so. Whatever was she thinking, to be babbling on about her mother so? And to a man who, no matter how devastatingly attractive, was a stranger. An English stranger. His eyes, those black, fathomless pools, the way he focused on her every word as if it were the most vital thing that had ever been said, they were enormously seductive. He made her quite long to tell him everything, every ugly secret she carried inside, to unburden her soul and move forward, free from guilt and pain and the whole rotten past. This man had enormous power, she sensed, but whether for good or evil she could not tell.

He was probably quite the rake back in England.

Just like someone else she knew.

It would be so very, very foolish to give him such power over her. If he was not to be trusted, then news of her whereabouts would find its way back to England so very quickly. Peter was still her legal guardian. He would come for her, drag her away from the tenuous happiness she had found for herself in Italy.

That Elizabeth could never bear. She could never go back to being Lady Elizabeth of Clifton Manor again. She had put all that behind her that awful night. The night she became a murderess.

It had been folly to even paint that portrait of Isobel Whitman Everdean, the Countess of Clifton, Incomparable, Diamond of the First Water, and mother. Anyone could have recognized her.

She would have to be very careful around this intense, unreachable man. She would be quite foolish to hire him, bring him into their household, make him privy to their secrets.

Really.

She couldn't do it. She could not!

"We were not speaking of my painting!" she snapped suddenly, turning her head away from her mother's smile, the smile that seemed to say *You are my daughter, after all.* Isobel had always had a keen eye for masculine beauty.

Nicholas seemed unfazed by her small fit of temper. He simply looked at her with faint amusement in his handsome eyes, and came to stand beside her. He towered above her, enveloping her in his warmth and the spicy scent of his soap, surrounding her in an inescapable cocoon of sheer maleness.

Not that she especially wanted to escape, she found.

"Were we not?" he mused, quite serene and unaware of her faintly gasping breath, the flush on her cheekbones. "And here I thought that your painting was the very reason I am here."

Elizabeth relented, and waved him to be seated on the chair beside hers. Anything so that he would cease looming over her, and she could think clearly again. "How did you discover I was in need of assistance?"

He shrugged. "Venice is small. One hears things."

So it was Georgie, Elizabeth thought. A small pang of unwelcome jealousy pierced her heart with the vision of her exquisite friend laughing and whispering with this man.

This man continued. "Despite what you may think, Miss Cheswood, I am in need of this position. I am a long way from home. Do you not want to help a fellow English patriot in need? A weak cripple, helpless and in need of an employment?" He brandished the silver-headed walking stick he had been leaning on.

He was about as helpless as a prowling lion on the savanna, Elizabeth knew, but oh, he was lovely, with that teasing gleam in his eyes. He swept his waving hair back from his forehead in one silky movement, and she almost melted into a puddle at his feet. A great, oozing puddle of female giddiness.

She also thought more pragmatically of the pile of unpaid bills stuffed into her desk drawers, of the hours of work that were going unrewarded because no one thought it important to pay a mere woman promptly. There were so many things she needed, such as pigments, canvas, new clothes. And she could not go on forever living on Georgina's generosity.

If anyone could get her rightful earnings quickly, it was this man.

Oh, but to see him every day! To look at him, talk to him, smell him. Could she do that, without throwing herself at him in some hoydenish fashion?

Could she?

Did she even have a choice in the matter? No. She did not.

Elizabeth rose and went to the unshuttered window, staring unseeing at the crowded alleyway below. Never, ever had she felt about a man as she did this one, this mysterious stranger with the roguish glint in his eye. There was something in him, an energy, that drew her inexorably.

She had always associated the sex act with her mother and stepfather's frequent noisy couplings and equally noisy screaming fits. With the rough hands of her ancient "fiancé" tearing at her clothes. With the intense way Peter would sometimes watch her, after he came back from Spain a sunburnt stranger. All of it had seemed so very repulsive. The few times she had become a bit tipsy and allowed Stephen or another artist to kiss her, she had been overwhelmed with fear and pushed them away. Even with Georgina's assurances of the joy of the act, she had not been convinced.

Elizabeth felt none of this fear around Nicholas. From the first instant she had glimpsed him in the Piazza San Marco, she had felt only delicious warmth, giddiness, like lying in the grass on a hot summer day. She had dreamed of him in her sleep after the ball, dreamed of kissing him. She had bitterly regretted the fact that they had been so rudely interrupted on the terrace.

Was she in truth becoming the "wanton artist" she

had been labeled by the more respectable society they had encountered?

She turned away from him now in abject confusion, her palms pressed to her hot cheeks. It was all so odd! Of all the men she had met in her travels, she should feel the least safe with this one. His presence was overwhelming in their narrow house, his silences intense and watchful, as if he waited for something from her. She knew almost nothing about him.

Nothing except the way she felt when he was near.

And for now, that was enough.

"Very well," she answered at last, turning back to him with a smile. "You are engaged."

He did not answer, merely watched her. His hands moved over the head of his walking stick.

"But you should know," she continued, "that I cannot afford to pay you until well, until after you begin your duties. I have no ready blunt at the moment." She had used the last of it on new ball gowns for Carnivale.

"Actually, Miss Cheswood," he interrupted, "you have something I would much prefer to ready blunt, until I have begun my duties and you are able to pay my wages."

Elizabeth stiffened. Had she misjudged this man after all? Was she not safe in his presence? She frowned. "What, pray tell, might that be, sirrah?"

But he surprised her yet again. "One of your paintings. Any you choose."

She felt her jaw begin to sag, and snapped it shut. "My paintings?"

"Yes. I have an idea they will be worth a great deal one day. If, however, you would rather not part with one..."

"No! I am quite willing to pay you in paintings. I

am simply surprised that you would choose that over coin."

He smiled at her again, that flash of white teeth and dimples that left her dazzled. "Maybe you should give me your account books to look over, Miss Cheswood, so I may begin my duties."

"I have one duty for you already."

"Indeed? And what might that be?"

She laughed at the naughty tilt of his grin. "Nothing terribly interesting, I'm afraid! You must call me Elizabeth."

"Only if you, in turn, call me Nicholas."

She nodded. "Done. We are very informal here, as you shall soon find."

As she went to retrieve the books from where she had shoved them beneath a table, Bianca came in bearing a tea tray, still wearing her bedsheet draperies. Her eyes rolled in approval at the handsome man, and she almost tripped over her train while trying to swing her hips in his direction.

Close on her heels was Georgina, a smart feathered bonnet on her auburn curls and a green velvet cloak folded over her arm. She clapped her gloved hands at the sight of the dusty ledgers. "Excellent, Lizzie!' she said. "I see you are finally showing good sense, and have hired Mr. Carter. So lovely to see you again, sir." She held out her fingers, and Nicholas gallantly raised them to his lips.

Wonderful, Elizabeth thought wryly, turning away from their giggling and smiling. Two unrepentant flirts in one household. And Georgie had even known his surname!

But the jealousy quickly melted away under her friend's familiar smile, her airy kiss on Elizabeth's cheek. "Now, dear, I must be off. After you have your tea, Bianca can show Nicholas to his room."

"R-room?" Elizabeth stuttered. Nicholas was to sleep here, under the same roof?

Oh, dear.

"Is that quite proper?" she asked.

"Oh, Lizzie, we are already a scandal! This one tiny thing cannot do us harm. And it is just the small room on the third floor. It will make things ever so much more convenient, will it not, Nicholas?" Georgina winked—winked!—at him.

"Oh, quite, Mrs. Beaumont." He winked back. Bianca wriggled and giggled.

Elizabeth almost moaned.

Then she laughed hysterically when the drawing room door banged open to reveal Stephen, whose face was every bit as red as his hair, except for some modeling clay stuck to his forehead.

"You!" he roared, pointing a trembling finger at the tea-sipping Nicholas. "What are you doing here, annoying these ladies?"

"Stevie, dear," Georgina clucked. "He is hardly annoying us. He is Elizabeth's new secretary." Then she poured herself a cup of tea, and sat back to watch the *commedia dell-arte* scene being played out in her very own drawing room.

Bianca snickered.

There was only one thing for a sensible girl like Elizabeth to do. She caught up her skirts and ran to the kitchen to fetch a pitcher of ice water to fling over their heads before they could destroy her drawing room.

NICHOLAS LEANED back on the narrow bed of his third-story room, examining the calling card Georgina Beaumont had pressed into his hand the night before —the card that had begun this entire crazy odyssey of playing secretary. It was almost dawn, and the drunken party who had congregated in the alleyway below his window had at last departed, leaving him alone in the grayish silence just before light.

God's blood, but this task had been meant to be so very simple! A spoiled miss who had imprudently fled the protection of her stepbrother, was to be found and summarily returned to where her best interests would be looked after. He was merely to snatch up the silly girl and deposit her back on Peter's doorstep before he could have time to become at all deeply involved in this Everdean family drama. His debt to Peter, long unpaid, would be canceled when he delivered the girl, and he could return to his old life in the gaming rooms and courtesans' boudoirs of London.

He had a good life. He did. He was wealthy, a member of several interesting if disreputable clubs, and despite his scar women were drawn to him. He was the despair of his high-stickler stepmama and the father who only wanted to forget the reminder of his wicked youth that Nicholas was. He needed no complications, even when the complication was as delectable as Lady Elizabeth.

Nicholas reached beneath his pillow and withdrew the miniature that Peter had entrusted him with.

Even in the dim half-light. her painted eyes glowed a pale silver, as misty and deceptive as a Yorkshire moor or a London morning.

He could not deceive himself much longer. He had thought this would be the most simple of tasks, a jaunt across Italy, a mere trifle after years of warfare in Spain. An elfin beauty Elizabeth might be, and not silly and spoiled as he had thought. But she was still Peter's sister, and for some unfathomable reason, he wanted her back in his house. It was Nicholas's task—his only task—to see that that happened.

And playing at being a secretary seemed the simplest way to accomplish that.

5

WHEN NICHOLAS CAME DOWNSTAIRS for breakfast, he was still a bit pale from his thought-filled night. Yet he managed a gallant bow and a bright smile.

"Good morning, Mrs. Beaumont. Miss Cheswood," he greeted. "It is obvious that nothing disturbed your beauty sleep. Venice could have no two fairer flowers in any of its gardens, by my faith."

It was a weak *bon mot* at best, but it made the women laugh, particularly Georgina. She waved him to the empty place setting at the small table, which was laden with plates of toast, pots of tea and chocolate, and small jars of marmalades and jellies.

"La, sir!" she said. "You obviously share my liking for the novels of the Minerva Press. I vow I read those very words in *Lady Charlotte's Revenge*. Quite an excellent work. Have you read it?"

"I fear I have not."

"I shall lend you a copy." Georgina poured out a cup of tea and passed it to him. "And did we not say you must call us Georgina and Elizabeth?"

"Indeed you must," said Elizabeth. She was engaged in buttering her toast, but paused to smile at him. "As you can see, we are hardly formal here."

Indeed they were not. Nicholas studied the small, sunny breakfast room while he sipped at the strong tea. Blank canvases were stacked along the walls, amid empty crates waiting for completed paintings to be packed in them and sent off to patrons. Plates and glasses were piled haphazardly on the sideboard, and linens peeked out of its almost-closed drawers.

Even the women's garments were unconventional. Georgina actually wore a dressing gown of burgundy velvet and had stuffed her auburn curls up into a snood, while Elizabeth was slightly more dressed in a yellow muslin round gown and paisley shawl.

Nicholas had never been in such a household. Even an army tent was carefully organized and regimented, and his mistresses' houses had been untidy and informal in a very studied way, their hair carefully coiffed even when they wore chemises.

This home was strange, almost exotic. It was wonderful.

"We were just discussing your first task," Elizabeth said, interrupting his ruminations.

"Oh, yes?" he answered. He smiled at her over the rim of his teacup.

She smiled in return, and blushed a very becoming peach. She even seemed more at ease with him this morning, after dousing him with water yesterday. Her eyes were clear and bright, her manner full of assurance.

She might very well be shy in matters of flirtation, but she was obviously a woman in full charge of her work. When she spoke of it, or even prepared to speak of it as she now did, her shoulders straightened and her cheeks grew bright with excitement.

"Yes," Elizabeth answered. "I did a very large charcoal sketch some months ago for Signor Visconti, of his children. I have not yet received the promised payment. If you can collect it, you will have made a very promising beginning indeed." She pushed a small stack of papers toward him. "Here is the contract, and a description of all dealings I have had with Signor Visconti."

Nicholas nodded, and placed the papers carefully inside his jacket. "I will see to it at once."

"You should be warned," Elizabeth added, "that Signor Visconti is a dreadful old miser. He would rather crawl on broken glass than part with a single sou."

"He is also an old lecher," interjected Georgina. "He pinched my backside at a ball last month, and I could not sit for a full day!"

Nicholas laughed. "Do not fear, fair ladies! I am certain I can deal very effectively with both the miser and the lecher."

"Well," said Elizabeth, "I shall certainly be eternally grateful if you do."

Nicholas merely smiled.

ELIZABETH WAS ACUTELY conscious of Nicholas hovering at her shoulder, watching her as she painted, for several long moments before she lowered the brush and turned to face him.

Her hand was trembling far too much, and the leaves on the sun-drenched trees of the canvas were beginning to look rain-hazy.

"Yes?" she said, trying not to appear too calf-eyed as she looked up at him.

"That is a lovely portrait," he answered. "It is almost complete?"

"Yes." Elizabeth eyed the little girl's likeness proudly. It was indeed some of her finest work yet. The child's mischief shone in the glowing colors. "Fortunately. Beatrice is a beautiful girl, but I do not think she is destined to be an artist's model. She is rather..."

"Hoydenish?"

"No!" Elizabeth laughed. "I believe 'spirited' was the word I wanted, but hoydenish is even more accurate. This portrait would have been finished a fortnight ago if she had not been up and into mischief every five minutes."

"If her doting mama had disciplined her, instead of sitting in the corner eating bonbons "

Elizabeth nodded wryly at the memory of Signora Farinelli's complete ineffectiveness. "I suppose, however, that it is a fond mama's way to be indulgent. Perhaps even overindulgent at times."

Nicholas's handsome face hardened, and he turned away. "Some mamas, perhaps."

Elizabeth's curiosity was piqued. "Yes. I know mine was, terribly. She let me wear party frocks all day long if I liked, and even let me drink from her wineglass at supper."

"Hmm."

"Yes. I was such a horrid brat." She wiped her hands on a rag and went to stand beside him, watching as he rifled through a pile of her sketches. "What was your mama like?"

He did not look up. "My mama?"

"Yes. Come now, you must have had one. I have serious doubts you sprang from your father's head fully grown, like Athena, and I am long past the age where I will be placated by stories of cabbage patches and storks."

ıhat finally won a reluctant smile from him. "Yes, I had a mama, for whatever she was worth. She was not very much at home."

"Oh." Elizabeth sighed sympathetically. "And I suppose you were sent off to a school very young, too."

"Oh, yes. A horrid school where they beat us with birch branches and forced us to take cold baths."

Elizabeth glanced suspiciously at the dimple that had appeared in his cheek. "I do believe you are telling me a Banbury tale, Nicholas!"

"Indeed I am. There were only ever warm baths at my school."

She sat down on the red velvet chaise she used for models, and drew him down beside her. "What school did you go to?"

"Not one you ever would have heard of."

Elizabeth did not hear the evasive tone in his voice at all. She was far too busy admiring how good his dark hair looked against the red velvet, and how very beautiful his long-fingered hands were. With his hair falling in waves to his shoulders he looked like some pagan god of old. Dionysus at the feast.

How she wanted to paint him! She would place him in some ancient ruins, wearing only a coronet of laurel leaves.

A giggle escaped before she could catch it.

"Is there something amusing?" he asked.

"No! No, I merely, well, um."

"What is it, Elizabeth?"

"Have you ever had your portrait painted, Nicholas?"

"You asked me that the night we met."

"Yes, but we were interrupted, before you could answer."

"Well, I have not. Except once in miniature."

"For a girl who waited while you went away to war?" A jealous pang pierced her heart.

His dimple froze, and disappeared. "What makes you think I was at war?"

Elizabeth shrugged. "That is usually the purpose of a miniature, in these times. And I have thought that you have something of the bearing of a soldier, even if you never sit up straight. And there is your scar."

She prodded at his slouched shoulders, and he immediately shot up poker-straight.

"Yes," he said, "I was at war. But that was a very long time ago, and I have applied myself most diligently to forgetting it."

"Yes. Of course."

They fell silent, listening to the sounds from the street and Bianca singing in the next room. Elizabeth was all-too conscious of the sound of his breathing, of the warmth of his leg against hers. She imagined reaching her hand out to him, touching the silky fall of his hair, pressing her lips to the dimple in his cheek.

She leaped up from the chaise.

"I-I just remembered an-an appointment." She gasped, not looking at him. "Very important. I must be going right away."

He stood up next to her, the sketches he had been looking at still in his hand. "I wanted to speak to you about the accounts."

"Yes, but I simply cannot now. I... I have to go!" She turned on her heel and whirled out of the room.

Nicholas watched her go, a bemused expression on his face.

"I ASKED Nicholas to accompany us to the opera, Lizzie."

Elizabeth paused in brushing the snarls from her black hair to tum and look at Georgina. Her friend was lounging on Elizabeth's bed, already dressed in her gown of gold tissue over bronze-colored silk, and eating chocolates.

"You did what?" Elizabeth said, her brow raised. "You asked him to go with us to the opera? But Stephen is escorting us! After the other day..."

Georgina kicked her bronze satin shoes in delight. "Wasn't it glorious, dear? Two men fighting over you, in our very own drawing room. It is just too bad you had to break it up like that, ruining the carpet with all that water."

Elizabeth tugged harder at the brush, yanking out several knots of hair in the process. "They smashed up two chairs, Georgie! And they are not even our chairs to break."

"Oh, pooh! They seem great friends now, Lizzie. Did you not see them talking at Lady Lonsdale's tea this afternoon? I only hope they can sober up enough to get us to the opera in one piece." Georgina slid off the bed and came to take over the brushing. "Here, let me do that or you will soon be quite bald, and that would never do. Not with the dashing Nicholas about."

Elizabeth smiled faintly, soothed by the hypnotic glide of the brush through her hair. "He is handsome, is he not?"

"*Mais oui*! I knew he would be perfect for you."

"Um-hm." Elizabeth couldn't help teasing just a bit. "He is going to straighten out accounts for me. Very useful."

"Pah! Lizzie, if you think all a man like that is useful for is accounts, then you do not deserve him. I have half a mind to steal him from you."

"Georgie!"

"I am only teasing, dear! He obviously belongs with you. I couldn't turn those marvelous dark eyes away from you if I ran through the Piazza San Marco in my chemise." Georgina laughed, and deftly twisted Elizabeth's hair up with black and silver ribbons. "Now, what will you wear?"

"That." Elizabeth threw off her dressing gown and picked up the black velvet and silk gown laid out on the bed.

Georgina clapped her hands. "Perfect! He will absolutely swoon when he sees you in that."

The black gown was quite the most daring thing Elizabeth had ever owned, bought on a whim in Rome and never worn. Transparent black tulle formed the long sleeves and draped at the décolletage, which dipped across the very rim of her bosom. If she were to so much as shrug, all her secrets would be revealed. It was as black and soft as the best kind of sin.

It was quite the gown a "scandalous artiste" would wear. And it was absolutely perfect for a gardenia-scented night in Venice.

Elizabeth had barely stepped into her black velvet

shoes when a slightly off-key rendition of *"Plaisirs d'amour"* floated up through the half-open window. Giggling, Georgina and Elizabeth threw open the casement and leaned out to see Nicholas and Stephen balanced precariously in a gondola, evening capes thrown back to facilitate their serenade. Nicholas held aloft a bottle of fine brandy in one hand, while the other held Stephen back from falling into the canal headfirst.

"What are you doing?" Elizabeth called. "I would wager some gondolier has reported his vessel stolen tonight!"

"Oh, lady fair!" Nicholas answered. "I assure you that your chariot was most honestly come by! And your loyal charioteers await your bidding."

Elizabeth laughed down helplessly as his white grin lit up the night.

She had never, ever felt so giddy, so reckless, so wonderful in all her life as she did this instant. An evening of revels ahead of her, a handsome man waiting to be her escort, and the most beautiful gown ever created on her back. She did not need a gondola—she could fly.

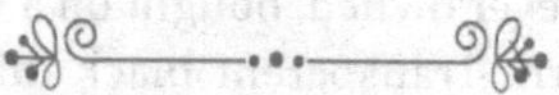

NICHOLAS DID ALMOST swoon when he glimpsed Elizabeth in her black gown. Black was supposedly only for mourning, but on her it gained a new life.

She leaned forward from the window, her creamy

bosom spilling from the bodice, and he very nearly pitched into the canal right beside the already-tipsy Stephen. She was all black and white, perfect elegance against the gray-pink stones of the house. She wore no jewels around her throat or in her ears, and only ribbons threaded through her hair, yet she shone.

During the long years in Spain, the months of waiting, he. had harbored a secret fantasy, one he could never have shared with his carousing friends, or even with Peter. He had dreamed of a woman, an Englishwoman, soft and sweet-scented and wide-eyed, who had smiled a secret, gentle smile only for him. He had dreamed of sharing laughter with this woman, of dancing with her under an English moon, of a gaiety untinged with desperation. This dream had kept him going when all seemed covered by dust and death.

Perhaps, when he had gone ceaselessly from party to party after his return from the war, he had been only seeking this dream woman. He had looked for her among English duchesses and English whores.

Yet he had had to travel to another land, to a place completely different from the England he knew, to a place of contradiction and enchantment, to find this dream. To see, in one fleeting moment, the truth of himself in the silver eyes of a woman who was as complex, as un-English, as Venice itself. Elizabeth Everdean was not at all what he had bargained for when he embarked from England on this wild chase.

She was certainly no milk-and-water miss, who would be easily led.

And then the brief flash of something was gone, as a whiff of incense on the breeze. Elizabeth waved down at him, then withdrew, shutting the window behind her. He was once again just a crippled bastard

Englishman, alone in a foreign city and playing a role that he sensed could quickly become most irksome.

Elizabeth, magical Elizabeth, was going to hate him so.

"I hope you have saved some of that brandy!" she cried gaily, emerging from the house engulfed in a black velvet cloak, her features hidden with a white half-mask.

"You are late." Stephen hiccoughed. But the hand he held out to assist her was steady enough.

"Pooh! The opera has not even started yet. And who arrives on time in Venice?" Georgina answered him. She leaped aboard in a flurry of spangled skirts, nearly capsizing them all. "Now, hand me that bottle, and row, my friends!"

Nicholas obeyed in silence, dipping his pole into water that now seemed as black and bitter as his own heart, and sent them off into the laughter-soaked night.

"ARE YOU NOT ENJOYING THE OPERA?" Elizabeth nudged her elbow into Nicholas's side, bringing his gaze from the stage where *The Coronation of Poppea* was being played out.

Things were becoming just the merest bit fuzzy around the edges from the two thimblefuls of brandy she had drunk, but even so she could see that he was troubled by something. There was a disturbing flatness to his eyes, a stillness about him when he always seemed to be in restless motion. At first she had feared that he disapproved of her, considered her the veriest hoyden in her daring gown and her brandy drinking.

It was more than that, though. He was acting just a bit like Peter had, when he had returned from the war so silent and searching and haunted.

She gave Nicholas her sunniest smile, and leaned gently against his shoulder. It was a lovely night, and she was bedamned if she was going to allow a man's dark mood to ruin it! "I can see you do not," she whispered. "But never fear, Mr. Carter. We shall go on to the Princessa Santorini's ball after, and it is certain to be livelier. I have heard she is to have living statues, naked and painted white. I intend to do a great deal of sketching while we are there."

A faint but promising gleam broke through the opaqueness of his eyes. He raised her gloveless fingers to his warm lips and kissed them, one by one. "This morning you called me Nicholas. And I am not entirely sure you could even hold a drawing pencil. That brandy was very potent."

Elizabeth sighed at the delicious feelings invoked by the touch of his lips. "Are you implying that I, a lady, am foxed, Nicholas?"

"Not a bit. No one could ever be drunk from the miniscule amount you had. A little happy, mayhap."

"Hmm." *I could be drunk on you*, she thought with a small smile. He tucked her hand into the crook of his arm, and she propped her chin on his shoulder. The feel of his soft hair against her cheek was absolute heaven. Deeply content, Elizabeth closed her eyes and listened to the music.

And reflected that never, if she had stayed in England and married into the ton as her brother wished, would she be allowed to behave so.

Suddenly, the music was interrupted by a brawl forming at the back of their box.

Georgina and Stephen had procured a bottle of champagne somewhere, and had begun the princessa's ball a bit early by steadily draining it. Now they were quarreling in fierce whispers.

Eventually Georgina lost her temper completely and actually pushed Stephen so hard he fell off his gilded chair with a resounding crash. Scandalized opera glasses turned in their direction, and even Nicholas was startled out of his sophistication enough to gape at them.

"It appears your suitor is being murdered by your sister," he murmured.

"Indeed." Elizabeth didn't even raise her head from his shoulder. "Georgie is my dearest friend in all the world, but at times she can be a bit, well, odd. I should absolutely know better than to take them about in public together. Something untoward always happens —a fire, a flood, a plague of locusts." She lifted one finger to his jaw and turned his eyes back to the stage. "Simply ignore them, and they will cease to make a spectacle of themselves."

The furor was indeed already dying down. Georgina had stopped giggling behind her fan, and helped Stephen to once again sit upright in his chair. He pretended to study the program.

Nicholas once again wondered just what he had embroiled himself in, getting involved with artists. Quarrels at the opera, maids dressed in bedsheets, what could happen next? His London friends were not precisely high sticklers for the proprieties, but this was something new again.

And once again, something fascinating.

"I do think they might have shared that champagne with us," Elizabeth whispered. She kicked at the empty bottle that had rolled beneath her chair. "It would have been the polite thing to do."

"Shall I go fetch you some?" he asked.

Elizabeth considered, weighing the empty bottle at her feet against the warmth of his shoulder beneath her cheek. She decided she should have both. "Only if you will agree to share it with me."

He pressed a quick kiss into her palm, and stood. "I will return soon. Do not move, and do not get into trouble."

She laughed aloud, unmindful of the stares being directed once more at their box. "I will not, Nanny." Somehow, Nicholas could not quite believe the angelic smile on her face.

"NICKY! Yoo-hoo Nicky!"

Nicholas groaned at the sound of that silver-bell voice, light tones straight from the deepest reaches of his nightmares. He would have fled into the crowd flowing in and out of the opera house if heavily bejeweled fingers had not already latched onto his arm. "It is you, Nicky!" Lady Evelyn Deake's violet eyes sparkled up at him from under darkened lashes. Her smile, carefully bright, was so brittle Nicholas almost expected her powdered cheeks to crack beneath it.

Long ago, when Nicholas had been newly home from Spain and feeling quite the monster with the red wound on his cheek and his stiff leg, Evelyn had briefly been his mistress.

He had been overly eager for a woman.

This was not at all a good thing. In point of fact, it was the very thing he had feared most, to encounter someone who had known him in London, before he could even decide what to do about Elizabeth. Though he should have realized it was a distinct possibility, with all the English who were flocking abroad.

But Evelyn Deake, of all people!

"Darling!" she cooed, smoothing back her golden ringlets. "I should have known it was you when I heard that someone was cavorting with those scandalous women artists. It is just your style!"

Nicholas debated pretending that he did not know Evelyn, that he had never heard of anyone called Nicholas, that he was Luigi and spoke no English. Yet even as the desperate thought flitted through his mind, he dismissed it. He deeply regretted his long ago, brief liaison with Evelyn, for now she knew him far too well to be put off by such flimsy deceptions. It would have to be a very good lie indeed to get past her.

"What a surprise, Evelyn," he said coolly, his dark lashes sweeping down to cover his dismay. He raised her jeweled hand, barely brushing the knuckles with his lips. "I would never have expected to see you in Italy. What can Lord Deake be thinking, to let himself be without your charming presence for so long?"

"You have not heard?" Evelyn fluttered her lacy fan and smiled her pointed cat's smile at him over its edge. "Dear Arthur went to his eternal reward last spring. Right in the very midst of the Season. Inconsiderate to the very end."

This explained the silvery gray of her gown. Evelyn used to favor the brightest reds and blues to be found in any modiste's. "My condolences. I had not heard. I was in Paris in the spring."

"Yes, so I heard. Political aspirations? Or merely wreaking havoc among all the little mademoiselles?"

Nicholas just bowed, as she trilled over her own wit.

"And now you have turned to the signorinas," she continued. "I suppose all the London beauties are wise to your charm now, Nicky."

Nicholas's gaze wandered over her shoulder to the handsome Venetian youth who stood a few feet from Evelyn, his Italian eyes practically smoldering with jealousy. "I see Italy is agreeing with you, Evelyn."

She threw a laughing glance at her escort. "You mean Alfredo? Yes, he is diverting. I am enjoying my stay in Venice enormously."

Nicholas forbore to point out how very mild the "scandalous" antics of Elizabeth and Georgina were in comparison with blatant dalliance with smooth-faced boys. "So you will be staying here for a time?"

She laughed again, that silvery artificial laugh that so grated on him. "My dear, I have purchased a house here. The *Ca Donati*. It is absolutely charming, if a trifle old, and, as you said, the Italians are treating me very well. I may never go back to London. Are you here for very long?"

Nicholas shrugged. "Only for a brief errand, I fear."

Evelyn pouted prettily. "How sad. I was so looking forward to renewing our acquaintance."

That would be when Venice sinks into the sea, he thought, but he said nothing and only swung his quizzing glass by its ribbon and watched her.

"But perhaps we can find time for a small tete-a-tete before you depart," she said.

"Can I confide a secret in you, Evelyn?" he asked, his voice low and intimate.

Evelyn swayed toward him. "Oh, yes, darling," she breathed. "I do so love secrets!"

Nicholas smiled inwardly in satisfaction. The queen of the scandal-broth had not changed a bit. "I am here incognito. On a wager."

"A wager? Oh, darling, how too delicious!" Evelyn giggled, obviously planning the many letters she would fire off to her friends back in England. "Can you tell me the particulars?"

"Not at present, I fear. But I do need your assistance."

"Of course, darling!" Evelyn put her hand on his arm, drawing so near that he was made nauseous by her sweet perfume.

"You must not divulge my identity to anyone. It would make the wager null and void."

He could almost see her mind spinning, longing for a glimpse of the betting book so far away in White's. "Do you mean no one in Venice knows your true identity but me?"

"No one but you, Evelyn."

"Not even Mrs. Beaumont and her little sister?"

"No." Especially not Mrs. Beaumont and her "little sister."

Evelyn laughed again. He gritted his teeth and smiled.

"Marvelous, Nicky! And of course you can count on my discretion. Only do tell me one thing."

"What?" he asked warily.

"Which sister is it? The widow or the little gypsy?"

Then Evelyn's gaze shifted, her smile turned sly. "Never mind, darling. I believe I can hazard a guess."

Nicholas looked back to see Elizabeth in the crowd, watching them, poised for flight. Her shocked face, openmouthed and wide-eyed, was at such odds with her daring gown that he almost laughed.

Almost.

"Hell and damnation," he muttered, and ran a shaking hand through his black curls. With a swift farewell, he broke away from Evelyn's grasp and rushed after Elizabeth's swiftly disappearing figure.

Evelyn's violet eyes narrowed as she watched him go.

6

ELIZABETH COULD NOT FORGET the image of Nicholas deep in conversation with the blond woman, their heads bent close as she looked up at him with dewy eyes and stroked his sleeve with her beringed hand.

Elizabeth had fled the opera house in confusion, leaving him behind in her mad dash to find a gondola to take her to the ball.

The princessa's ball was delightful. She did indeed have living statues, though artfully draped in loincloths rather than completely nude, and there was an abundance of champagne. Georgina and Stephen had left off their arguing by the time they caught up with her, and all her artist friends were there and bombarding her with questions about her coveted Katerina Bruni commission. Nicholas, who had at last shown up on his own, was quite attentive, bringing her delicacies from the supper buffet and dancing with her awkwardly on his stiff leg.

It should have all been quite perfect, and would have been if she could have forgotten about the woman at the opera house, ceased wondering who she was, what they had been discussing so intimately.

She was not jealous. She wasn't. How could she possibly be? She did not even really know Nicholas. He was her employee, her secretary. A very tall, very attractive secretary, to be sure.

Perhaps therein lay the difficulty, a tiny voice whispered in her mind. She did not really know Nicholas, and she wanted to. Very much.

All she truly knew was that he was English, and by his voice and manners, not of a lower class. An impoverished or adventurous younger son of gentry, perhaps.

She had no idea of what his past held, how he had really come by his scar, what had driven him to seek employment in their eccentric household. He could be a criminal, though she sensed this was not so.

Elizabeth wanted to know all these things. She wanted to pierce the armor of his reticence, see past his dark eyes, know his secrets. She had always been deeply curious, and he was by far the most intriguing mystery she had ever encountered.

But knowledge could come with a high price—the revelation of her own secrets. That she was a runaway, a murderess. And that was a price she simply could not pay, not even to satisfy that burning curiosity.

What a conundrum! She almost wished she had never seen him at all, never been faced with this dizzying jumble of jealousy, curiosity, excitement, lust, fear. She had been happy before, traveling and honing her craft, and not feeling so lost and lonely as she had in England. Yet if she had never met him. she would never have heard his laugh, seen his dimple when he smiled, or watched the admiration in his eyes when. he looked at her work.

Elizabeth buried her face in her hands, the music

and champagne and confusion making her head ache abominably.

"Lizzie, are you ill?" Georgina laid her cool hand against Elizabeth's brow. "You feel overly warm."

Elizabeth managed a small smile. "I am just tired, Georgie. Truly."

"*Pauvre petite*! You have been working too hard, and here I have dragged you about to too many parties this week. Shall we go home?"

"No. You are having such a good time, I could never forgive myself if I took you away so early."

Georgina bit her lip. "I'll fetch Nicholas to take you home, shall I?"

"No! Not Nicholas. He is dancing with our hostess, see? I can go alone. It is not far."

"Alone? In Venice? I should say not!" Georgina tapped her chin thoughtfully. "I shall get your fussy old Stephen to see us both home, then, and I will come back when you are settled. Yes?"

Elizabeth nodded in relief. She was aching for her bed, for dreamless sleep, for a cessation of the mad whirl of thoughts in her head. "Yes."

But their escape was not to be so easy. As they prepared to step into the gondola that would carry them home, a silvery voice called "Yoo-hoo! Oh, are you going toward the Giudecca Canal? May we ride with you?"

Elizabeth groaned and shrank back into the hood of her cloak.

It was the golden-haired woman Nicholas had been speaking with at the opera, and with her a glowering, beautiful young Venetian man. The woman was waving and coming toward them. It was all far too much a coincidence. Elizabeth had never seen this woman before in her life, and now here she was, twice in the same night.

And Georgina was smiling and saying that that was precisely the direction in which they were going.

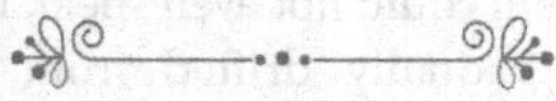

Lady Evelyn Deake was just the sort of English that Elizabeth most disliked encountering abroad. And not simply because she had been seen in intimate conversation with the all-too-alluring Nicholas, either. Their journey home, though not a great distance, was made longer by crowds of vessels filled with merrymakers. The shouts and screams and loud music were causing Elizabeth's head to throb, and Lady Deake's conversation was only making the situation worse. Even Georgina, usually so adept at deflating British pomposity, was only able to stare at Lady Deake in amazement while occasionally rolling her eyes in Elizabeth's direction.

Lady Deake had apparently been in Italy for several months, since the death of her "dearest Arthur," and found nothing to be to her exacting standards (except, to all appearances, for the sullen-mouthed Alfredo, whose hand never left her leg). She chattered about her home in London, which was ever so much larger and brighter and grander in every way than the crumbling old Ca Donati, which she recently purchased from the very disagreeable Marchese Donati. The servants in her London home were also a great deal more efficient than these lazy, dark Italians, who lounged about all day doing absolutely nothing to earn their wages. Italian food was so very upsetting to the digestion, and Italian women knew nothing about fashion (this said with long glances at Elizabeth's and Georgina's gowns), and some of them could not even speak English.

Elizabeth gradually drifted from the vivacious stream of complaints, leaning back on the cushions and studying the masked and costumed figures of the other groups, who were unfairly having fun. She had heard similar opinions many times, from English travelers from Milan to Messina, and now she merely smiled at Lady Deake while not hearing a single word she was saying.

She longed to, just this once, lose her temper and snap, *Cease your prattling at once, you silly woman!*

Unfortunately, she was no longer Lady Elizabeth Everdean, sister of the Earl of Clifton. She was Elizabeth Cheswood, scandalous artist who had to earn her bread. And she had heard of the Veronese fresco cycle in the Ca Donati, which was in dire need of restoration. Rumor had it that the new owner, now revealed to be Lady Deake, was looking for an artist to complete the task. It was a plum of a commission, and Elizabeth had wanted it.

Truth be told, she still wanted it.

She was quite aching to get her brushes on the Veronese, and that was the only thing that kept the prattling Lady Deake from plunging headfirst into the canal at Elizabeth's hands. That and her curiosity about Nicholas.

"... do you, Miss Cheswood?"

Elizabeth blinked at the sound of her name, floating back down into the reality of their overcrowded gondola and the overpowering scent of the other woman's perfume. "I beg your pardon, Lady Deake?"

Evelyn tittered. "Lost in some artistic rapture, no doubt, Miss Cheswood!"

"Um, quite."

"Venice is so full of scope for the imagination."

Elizabeth somehow doubted that Lady Deake's imaginative scope had ever gone any further than matching bonnet to redingote, but she merely nodded and tried to look romantically artistic.

Evelyn continued. "I was just asking what you, as another Englishwoman, have found most intriguing about the Italian landscape."

Elizabeth thought of Nicholas's velvet dark eyes, and blurted, "The men."

Evelyn tittered again, running one polished fingertip along Alfredo's arm. "Oh, yes, I quite agree! Englishmen have nothing to the mystery of the Italians." She smirked. "Most Englishmen, that is."

The gondola at last bumped to a halt before the looming shape of the Ca Donati, and they were soon on their way again, sans two passengers, amidst a trilled "*Ciao!*" from Lady Deake. Elizabeth was not sure if she was profoundly relieved or rather disappointed. The conversation had just been growing interesting.

Georgina burst out laughing as soon as the great brass doors shut behind Evelyn and her Italian. Elizabeth fell against her in helpless mirth, the two of them chorusing "*Ciao!*" under Stephen's bewildered gaze.

"I thought she was very... vivacious," he said.

That only made them laugh louder, the gondola swaying with the force of their hilarity.

"Oh, the mystery of Italian men!" Georgina simpered. "Not as tidy as Englishmen, of course, and so dark, but what eyes, what hands!"

"What backsides!" Elizabeth crowed. "But, Georgie, you were the one who let her accompany us. This is all on your head."

"Someone at the ball told me she was the new owner of the Ca Donati, and I wanted to hear about her Veronese. But alas, the woman is too silly to realize what she has." Georgina sighed. "Lady Deake quite reminds me of why I left England in the first place. How do those London misses ever tolerate it, Lizzie? All that money—all that lack of sense."

"I never was a London miss, Georgie, just a country mouse. After you left Miss Thompson's School to run away with Jack, I never had any excitement at all. The same people, the same parties, all the time." Elizabeth closed her eyes, listening to the soft slap of the oars in the water, the laughter all around her. The sweet-sick smell of the canal, smoky torches, perfumes, and flowers was thick in her throat and nostrils. She was suffused with Italy, and England, the place of secrets and silly people like Lady Deake, seemed quite far away.

Or perhaps too dangerously close.

Elizabeth inadvertently cried out in panic, pressing her fist against her mouth.

"Lizzie!" Georgina cried, reaching for Elizabeth's cold hand. "What is it? Are you feeling ill again?"

"No, no, nothing like that." Elizabeth tried to smile reassuringly. "It is only—oh, Georgie, promise me we will never leave this place! Never go back to England."

"Dearest, what has brought this on? Is it merely Lady Deake and her prattling? Or have you heard from your brother and you did not tell me?"

Elizabeth shook her head. "I did not mean to

alarm you, dear. I simply love our life here so. I like not having to be so careful all the time of what I say or do, for fear of being censured by some dowdy old duchess. I like wearing gowns like this one instead of fusty pastels, and drinking champagne, and painting all day." She broke off in a sob.

"Lizzie! Shh!" Georgina gathered her into a hug. "It will not change. We will never go back. Even if we did return to England, as we very well may one day, it would not be like that again. We are different. We will always be free."

"Promise me?"

"I promise. Why do you think I ran away with Jack all those years ago?"

Elizabeth sniffed, and gave a watery smile. "His dashing red regimentals?"

"Well, yes. But more than that, he offered to take me away from the tedium of Miss Thompson's and away to Portugal. You were the only bright spot in that gray cloister, Lizzie, and I was soon to finish and leave you anyway." Georgina patted her hand consolingly. "It is only that silly Lady Deake upsetting you. But you are safe here, Lizzie."

"Safe," Elizabeth whispered. "Yes."

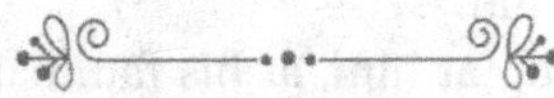

THAT NIGHT, for the first time in many months, Elizabeth dreamed of Clifton Manor. Of Peter.

It was hardly surprising, since she had been

dwelling on England and the past so much of late. Not even a glass of warm milk liberally laced with brandy had been able to help tonight, and all those memories came flooding up from where she had so firmly pressed them down and down.

In her dream, she was eighteen again, filled with youthful passion for her art, wild dreams of escaping Derbyshire and running off to a Parisian garret (as soon as Boney could be persuaded to quit the country and make its garrets safe for Englishwomen). The countryside was dull, there was no one to talk with but their neighbors, the giggling spinster Misses Allan and old Lady Haversham, and Peter always seemed so angry with her. Angry, and cold, and beautiful as an ice storm.

In the beginning of this dream, he came to her again in her makeshift studio, sunlight all around them from the high, unshuttered windows. His long fingers were hard on her arms, biting into the soft flesh bared by her puffed-sleeved gown, but she hardly felt it. His voice, rough and low, unrecognizable from his usual patrician tones, came to her as if from a very far distance.

"I cannot bear it any longer." He gasped. "You were put here just to torment me, Spanish harlot. The way you look at me, the way you talk." His eyes swept over her. "Just as she did."

She stared up at him, at his familiar features distorted in almost-painful passion, at the way the sun turned the silver gilt of his hair to a halo. She was shocked, numb, utterly stricken. She wanted to scream, to cry, to run, but she was paralyzed. She could only stand there in his grasp.

His hands pulled her against him, raising her on tiptoe so that his watch chain pressed into her tender belly. His breath was warm as his lips trailed across her cheek.

"No!" she cried out, her voice dismayingly faint. "No, this is wrong. You are my brother!"

"What new trick is this? Your brother?"

And she knew then that he did not see her, Elizabeth. But she did not know what it was he did see. She broke free, running behind her easel, her breath bursting from her.

"Then you will have to marry someone else," he murmured, almost to himself. "You must go away from here, because I cannot look at you anymore."

He reached for her again, but his long, pale hand became the Duke of Leonard's twisted, arthritic claw, pinching at her. She looked up at Peter, but his face was horrible now, wrinkled, the spittle flying from the corner of his mouth as he cackled, "Whore! Murderess!"

She heard a woman's shrill laughter, and looked to see Lady Deake, golden and perfect in a white gown, laughing with malice.

The spittle at the duke's mouth became blood, a great scarlet flood of it, and she was drowning, drowning, awash in the blood and guilt and fear. Drowning.

Elizabeth came awake with a gasp, sitting straight up amid her twisted sheets. A Venetian moon lit up even the corners of her small room, revealing only the benevolent clutter of gowns and hats and canvases.

The duke was long dead, and Peter was very far away.

"Oh," she whispered, and fell back against her pillows. "Oh."

She had to laugh, once her heart slowed in her breast. It was quite ridiculous, really, to become so overwrought over a dream vision of the duke and

Lady Deake behaving like bad street fair players. Silly.

If only that horrid scene in her studio at Clifton Manor had not really happened, once in another lifetime. If only she could forget it now.

If only she did not truly have blood on her hands. Elizabeth lay on her wide, white-curtained bed, the blankets kicked into a heap at her feet, moonlight and a cold breeze flowing from the open window, her eyes focused on the plastered ceiling above her. And she allowed all those memories to wash over her, the beautiful ones along with the ugly. She let herself be Lady Elizabeth Everdean again.

7

ELIZABETH HAD BEEN SIX years old when her mother, Isobel, a dashing widow and a true Diamond of the First Water, had left merry widowhood behind to marry the equally dashing Charles Everdean, the Earl of Clifton. Only six when they left their crowded town house for Clifton Manor, and what Isobel called "Your new father and brother, darling."

Elizabeth had liked Charles, who had allowed her to take his name, and she had idolized Peter. Twelve years her senior, he had been everything she could have wanted in an elder brother. He had taught her to ride her pony, had read her books from the vast Clifton library, had protected her from their parents' many noisy quarrels.

After Isobel and Charles died when Charles's high perch phaeton had overturned during a race, Peter had cared for her tenderly. Mourned with her, encouraged her budding interest in art, arranged for her education at Miss Thompson's School, and even taken her to London once to visit the Elgin Marbles. Then he had purchased his commission and been off to Spain, to be shot at and send her infrequent letters. Until the letters trickled to a mere handful, and then ceased altogether.

When he returned, he had not been at all the same Peter. Her golden, laughing brother had been replaced by a bitter stranger. A stranger who drank far too much, who lurked in his dark library, and forbade her to give parties, until her very few local friends dropped away. A stranger who stared at her with glowing blue eyes and yet seemed not to see her. He even provoked quarrels with her, until the temper she had inherited from Isobel would loom up, and she would scream and throw things like the veriest fishwife.

After that horrid scene in her studio, Elizabeth realized she could not live with Peter any longer. She agreed to the betrothal with the Duke of Leonard, some political crony of Peter's, only to escape, thinking that nothing could be worse than the prison Clifton Manor had become.

How very, very wrong she had been.

Elizabeth was torn from her memories by a sound from the small terrace outside her open window. The tap of a cane, as soft as cat's paws. She pushed back the blankets and slid out of bed, threw on her dressing gown, and crept outside.

"Hello, Nicholas," she said, somehow not at all surprised to see him awake so far past the witching hour. There was, after all, a sort of fatedness about a moonlit night during Carnivale that made all things seem possible.

He was barefoot, clad only in an open shirt and black trousers as he leaned back against the marble balustrade. The red tip of his thin cigar glowed in the darkness, and the moonlight gleamed off the half-empty crystal snifter of brandy balanced next to him.

The night was chill, but he did not seem to feel it, and neither did she.

"I did not mean to wake you," he said, his voice rough with smoke and brandy. "Georgina said you were feeling unwell."

"I am feeling much better. And I was already awake." Elizabeth saw the brandy, and gestured toward it. "May I?"

He wordlessly held the snifter out to her. They stood in companionable silence, with Nicholas looking down at the canal and Elizabeth looking at his bare chest. At the way the light dusting of black hair across the smooth muscles disappeared into his waistband. His skin looked like Georgina's gold satin dress, and Elizabeth longed to rub her palm across it and see if it was as sleek as it looked, to press her lips against the joining of his neck and collarbone. She wanted to bury her nose in that hair and inhale deeply of his clean, spicy scent.

That clean smell that seemed to wash away all the wickedness she had seen.

Elizabeth shook her head fiercely to clear it. "I had such dreams," she said. "I could not go back to sleep."

Nicholas took a long sip of brandy before he answered. "It is this place."

"This place?"

"Venice." He waved the red glow of his cigar at the houses, sleeping pale gray in the twilight. "There is witchcraft in it. It must have enchanted your dreams."

She was startled. She would never have thought him the poetic sort. Intelligent, flirtatious, and even appreciative of art, yes. But not poetic. "That it has. But a very good sort of enchantment."

"Even though it disturbs your sleep?" "Even then."

"And the same enchantment is not to be found in England?"

"No. That is exactly why I love it here. It is like no place else—especially not England."

"Do you ever think of going back there?" he asked. "To your home?"

Elizabeth narrowed her eyes as she looked at him. There was a sort of tension in him now, a stillness, a waiting. This was not just idle chatter, she felt. He wanted something from her, wanted her to say something, but she could not begin to fathom what. She reached for his brandy and took another fortifying swallow before she answered. "I am home."

"Yet surely you miss England. Surely your life there was easier than it is here, wandering like a nomad," he pressed.

"Easier!" The memory of her recent dream, of Peter and the dead duke, was still fresh and powerful, and she lashed out at this gorgeous man who seemed strangely intent on bringing all that ugliness into the light. "Easy, to be nothing but a prisoner, to be helpless and never free to be myself? You know nothing of me, Nicholas, or my life in England. You don't know what it was like when Georgina left. You don't know what Italy, what being here, means to me."

"No," he answered quietly. "I do not."

"No." Elizabeth was suddenly tired, achingly tired to her very toes. And appalled at how very much she had almost revealed.

"Will you tell me, Elizabeth?"

"Tell you?"

"About your life in England." He placed his hand over hers where it rested on the balustrade, his palm warm and comforting. He was a cipher to her, but he was so large and solid. It was tempting, just for a moment, to lean against him and put all her worries onto those wide shoulders.

But only for a moment. To give up her hard-won independence would be so dangerous. What if this man came to hear of what she had done? He would hate her, and could even turn her in to the authorities.

She wiped at her damp cheeks, and stepped away from his tempting warmth.

"Please," he said softly. "I want to know."

"There is not much to tell," she answered, forcing a lightness she was far from feeling into her tone. "I had a very ordinary life there, one some women would find enviable."

"Not you." It was not a question.

"No. I could not breathe," she admitted. "I was drowning. I had to leave, or lose myself completely. I had a certain security, but it was not enough."

"You had family there?" His voice was tight.

For an instant, Elizabeth thought of Peter as he had once been, golden bright and laughing, swinging her into the air to hear her childish giggles. She shook her head. "No. Georgie is my only family."

"You left a secure life in England for the uncertainties of a life abroad? You and your sister?"

"Yes. It sounds insane, I know. Perhaps it is insane."

"No. Not insane. I understand the need to escape."

Elizabeth studied the glow of his eyes in the night, and somehow she knew. "You do understand. You understand why I left comfortable respectability to become an artist, a professional artist and not some drawing room dabbler. Why I won't go back."

He gave a sharp bark of singularly humorless

laughter. "Respectability is quite overvalued, my dear. You were absolutely correct to run in the opposite direction."

"Is that what you are doing, Nicholas? Running from something?"

"Isn't everyone doing that, in one way or another?"

"Yes. But everyone's 'something' is different." Elizabeth turned to him, giving in to the temptation to place her palm against his skin, against the strong beat of his heart. "What is your something, Nicholas? What are you running from? And what does your heart want more than anything else?"

"I do not know." He put his hand over hers, pressing her paint-stained fingers into his skin. "Perhaps to escape from myself. To cease being myself, for just one day, and become someone better."

"I told you why I left England," she whispered. "Will you tell me why you left?"

"I was searching for something. A lost object."

"What was it?"

He smiled crookedly. "Maybe it was you, sweet Elizabeth."

She tried to push back. "Don't tease."

He held her, refusing to let her leave. "I am not teasing. Far from it."

Then he bent his head and kissed her, softly at first, his cool lips barely brushing hers. But when she offered no objection, he deepened the pressure, bending her back over his arm as he kissed her deeply, warmly, seekingly. She had never, ever been kissed like this before, and it was utterly delicious.

Elizabeth finally drew back slightly, drawing the breath deeply into her starved lungs. She stared up at him, dazed. Slowly, details like the cold marble balustrade against her back, his hand on her hip, began to penetrate the pink haze of her passion.

She trailed one fingertip over his features, his glistening lips, the pale scar. "Oh, Nicholas," she breathed, unable to say anything else. "Oh, Nicholas."

8

"SO LOVELY, CARA! *Molto bene*," Katerina Bruni, the famous courtesan, purred. She stretched on the red velvet chaise, her emerald eyes never leaving the figure of Nicholas, who was bent over the account books at Elizabeth's desk and taking no notice of anything else.

Even when the loose sleeve of Katerina's blue velvet robe slid off her shoulder and she took her own time shrugging it back into place.

Elizabeth couldn't help but giggle just a little. She turned away to mix a bit more of the blue pigment.

"Where did you discover him, Signorina Cheswood?" Katerina continued. "I never saw him before the princessa's ball last night."

"And you know every man in Italy?" Elizabeth teased.

Katerina laughed. "I do, I do! All the ones worth knowing. It is my business. But your new—secretary, is it?"

"Yes."

"He is something different. Very handsome, very mysterious." Katerina tapped at her chin with one pink fingernail. "Yet very serious at the moment. Must be English, no?"

Elizabeth giggled again. Nicholas, serious? She truly liked Katerina Bruni, not something to be said for most of her clients. Signora Bruni showed up as scheduled for her sittings, sat still, and her "patron" always paid the bills on time. She was also an amusing conversationalist, and Elizabeth valued her opinions on men and business. But obviously her powers of observation were not so acute where Nicholas was concerned.

"He is English. But, between us..." Her voice dropped to a whisper. "Seriousness is not among his many qualities."

It was Katerina's turn to laugh. She covered her mouth with her white feather fan, the sapphires in its handle catching the sunlight from the windows. "So what are some of the qualities he does possess? Or is that too, um, private?"

Elizabeth thought of the previous night, of their kiss on the terrace, of his hands on her back, his lips warm and soft on hers. She could feel her cheeks pinkening. "Oh, assuredly private, Signora Bruni!"

Katerina pouted a bit. "*Cara!* And after all I have told you about the marquis. Am I not your friend?"

"Well..." Elizabeth glanced at Nicholas from the corner of her eye. "He does have the grandest..."

"Is there something amusing over there, ladies?" Nicholas called out.

Elizabeth and Katerina both started guiltily and looked away. Katerina fanned herself vigorously, and Elizabeth busied herself mixing more pigment.

"Oh, not at all!" she answered. "Signora Bruni was just telling me a bit of interesting gossip she heard at the ball last night."

"Oh? And would you care to share it?"

He sounded so very much like the stern Miss Thompson at her old school that Elizabeth laughed out loud again. When she turned to him to share this, however, he looked so very forbidding that she merely shook her head. "It would not interest you, Nicholas."

"Hmm." He shut the account book he had been perusing, and rose to his feet. "I must run an errand. I will see you after tea."

Elizabeth frowned. "Very well. Don't forget about the Vincenzis' party tonight."

"I will not. Good afternoon, Elizabeth. Signora Bruni." He bowed, and was gone.

"Now then, Signorina Cheswood," Katerina said. "He is gone, and you can tell me all. Is that *dolce* man your lover? And if he is not, would you object if I tried my luck?"

"No!" Elizabeth cried, appalled at the thought of Nicholas in the very alluring arms of Signora Bruni. "Well, that is, he is not my lover. Not precisely. We have kissed, that is all."

"Ah, but some kisses are enough, yes?"

"I... yes. Some kisses are quite enough." Elizabeth shook her head. She had not stuttered so very much since she had learned to talk.

"Then," Katerina continued, "you must want him as your lover."

"No. I..." *I want him as my husband.* Elizabeth almost dropped her paintbrush in shock at the unbidden thought. As it was, she trailed a long streak of blue over the creamy expanse of painted shoulder.

"I see." Katerina nodded wisely. "Well, cara, it is simple enough. I shall loan you one of my black silk chemises. They are always successful."

Elizabeth placed the brush carefully into the jar of

turpentine, her hands shaking so much she feared for the rest of the painting.

"Are we finished for the day, Signora Bruni?" she said.

"Hmm? Oh, yes, I must be at the dressmaker's in half an hour. Shall I see you on Tuesday?"

"Yes, Tuesday."

After Katerina had departed, Elizabeth busied herself tidying up, cleaning off the ugly blue streak, but her mind was miles away.

Nicholas, a husband? She, Elizabeth, a wife? It was such an absurd idea!

She had vowed never to marry, to put her art first. Now here were visions of country churches. And large, cozy marriage beds.

"Stop that right this moment!" she told herself sternly, as she struggled to push the chaise back against the wall. "You are being a nodcock, and it must cease now before it begins to affect your work."

She collapsed onto the chaise, and stared up at the ceiling in utter confusion.

All the worry and fuss was probably for naught, anyway. Nicholas had been very distant and preoccupied ever since he had come to breakfast that morning, not looking at her, not speaking to her directly if he could avoid it. He seemed, in point of fact, to be thinking of something far away, and not her and what had happened between them at all.

That kiss, that wonderful, glorious kiss had obviously not affected him as it had her. She had longed to run to him as soon as she awoke that morning, to feel his arms around her, keeping her safe.

He had appeared to want to run *from* her. "Perhaps I made far too much of a small thing," she mused aloud.

That was, unfortunately, entirely possible. She did not have the experience Nicholas did. What was earth-moving to her was probably a mere diversion to him, a pleasant interlude.

"Oh!" she whispered in abject confusion. "Why can love not be simple?"

She needed advice badly.

BENNO ("NO LAST NAMES, SIGNOR") was a very disreputable character indeed. His hair fell in greasy black hanks from beneath a battered hat; his coat was full of holes; and his stench rivaled that of the fetid alley where Nicholas stood speaking with him. Still, Benno did seem to know his business. And he had been highly recommended by the people Nicholas had been talking to in the tavernas in the previous days.

"So, signor." Benno's bloodshot gaze shifted around them, always searching. "You require a kidnapping. Of a lady."

Nicholas did not at all like the way Benno licked his lips at the mention of the word *lady*. "I require assistance at a kidnapping. I will stay with the lady the entire time."

"Eh?" Benno's eyes narrowed in disappointment. "Then what do you need Benno for, if you do it all yourself?"

"You are more familiar with Venice, the back ways,

the more flexible officials. I need assistance in making certain the lady is taken safely out of Venice, out of Italy, without being detected by her friends."

"Benno does know the back ways of Venice, true." His grimy face still reflected dismay at the loss of being alone with his abductee. Yet other, more mercenary, concerns soon took over his disappointment. "Benno does not come cheap, signor."

"No, indeed. I never supposed Benno did." Nicholas reached into his many-caped greatcoat and withdrew a hefty purse, clinking invitingly with coins. Benno snatched at it, but Nicholas deftly held it out of his reach. "This is a small payment. There will be another purse when our task is complete and the lady is out of Italy."

"Signor—"

"If you accept this payment, Benno, I expect service. If you take it into your head to cheat me, I will find you and you will regret it. Are we understood?"

"Oh, yes, signor, yes! Benno would never cheat you. Never. I am an honest businessman."

An honest extortionist and kidnapper. How novel. "Good. See that you remain so." Nicholas delivered the purse into Benno's eager hands. "Then listen closely. This is what I require. I want a gondola, a covered gondola, waiting tomorrow afternoon at a location I will send you word of. I will need blankets, and a quantity of laudanum."

"Oh, yes, signor. Benno will take care of it all."

"Excellent. Now get out of here. I will send you word shortly."

Benno's shuffling footsteps soon died away, and Nicholas was alone in the dark, stinking alleyway. But he did not see the tottering piles of refuse, or the rats who peered at him from the shadows. He only saw

Elizabeth, as she had been on the terrace, pale in the moonlight, smiling up at him after he had kissed her so improperly.

He felt again the way she had leaned into him, the way her mouth fit so perfectly with his. The cool silk of her hair in his fingers. The trust shimmering in her eyes.

She was extraordinary, unlike any woman he had ever known before. Sophisticated, but with a glowing innocence still in her eyes, alluring and beautiful, but totally unaware of it. The way she moved and laughed and thought was utterly unique. He could have spent months, years, watching her, studying her, and still never have discovered all the facets of her. She was always surprising him.

He knew she would be beautiful and fascinating when she was ninety.

And it was when he realized this, last night, that he had known he had to move. He had to make this business over and finished before he could not do it at all. Before he snatched up Elizabeth and ran with her, to Turkey or China or America, or any place where they would never be found and where he could spend all his days watching her.

He had to forget about her. He had to think only of Peter, and his promise. He owed the man his life! And all Peter wanted in exchange was... Nicholas's very heart.

"Elizabeth," he whispered. "My dear. I am so very, very sorry."

But only the rats were there to hear him, to watch him cry for the first time in years. The first time since he had been told Peter was dead in Spain.

THAT AFTERNOON, with no warning, the heavens opened and a deluge poured down. And Venice was impossibly dismal.

Georgina lay on the settee, wrapped in her warmest dressing gown after being caught in the rain on her way home from a sitting, and became engrossed in the latest horrid novel from England. Elizabeth sat in her comer, attempting to work some more on the Katerina Bruni portrait. Her brush moved over the canvas methodically, but she could not seem to concentrate on the courtesan's pouting expression, or on giving her green eyes the sparkle that was so much a part of her.

Elizabeth's thoughts kept flying to the kiss again, and Nicholas's strong shoulders beneath her hands. When she tried to shade a long curl, she instead saw him, smiling down at her as they floated on a sun-drenched canal while he tried to steer their gondola. Her brush moved of its own accord, and she soon found she had painted in the margins of the canvas, not the dusky Katerina, but a laughing Nicholas.

"Oh, no!" Elizabeth stared aghast at her painting. "This must cease!"

"What?" Georgina looked up from her book. "Did you say something, Lizzie?"

Elizabeth tossed her brush aside and went to look out the window at the unceasing rain. The gray torrent had driven all the merrymakers indoors, and the city was deserted. Only a few bedraggled streamers and blossoms gave a tiny splash of color.

"I said this rain has to cease," she said, tracing one fingernail through the mist on the windowpane. "Or it will ruin the Vincenzis' party tonight."

"Indeed, it was meant to be in their grand gardens. Such a shame if it is spoiled, and you do not get to dance under the stars with the divine Nicholas!"

"Oh, Georgie, really." Elizabeth's rebuke was faint. She had daydreamed of dancing under a star-strewn sky in Nicholas's strong arms.

"Is that all that is worrying you, Lizzie?" Georgina put her book aside, and sat up.

"What else could it be?"

"I do not know. Nicholas? The two of you looked so happy at the opera yesterday. You could not stop looking at each other."

"Oh, yes, it was lovely!" Elizabeth paused. "And... and last night, he kissed me."

"Lizzie, how marvelous!"

"Yes. Marvelous." Elizabeth's voice was small, even to her own ears.

"Then what is wrong, dear? You are attracted to him, he is attracted to you, you are spending time together."

Elizabeth left the window and went to sit next to her friend, tucking an extra lap robe around her chilled shoulders. "Georgie, I need your help."

"Whatever you need, Lizzie. You only need ask."

"I need you to tell me about your marriages."

Georgina's eyes widened. "My marriages? But, Lizzie, you know all about them! And none of them lasted long enough to be really interesting."

"I know their names, but I do not know about them. About your feelings for them. Your letters when we were apart were always about your work, the people you were meeting. Never about your husbands."

"Well." The unflappable Georgina Beaumont somehow seemed at a loss for words. Her mouth opened and closed a few times before she spoke again. "Well, Lizzie, you know I will tell you whatever you want to know, but why this sudden desire to know this?"

"I do not know! I thought perhaps, oh, this is so foolish. I-I wish to know more about men."

"Oh." Georgina fell back against her pillows. "But, Lizzie, you know about men! There is Stephen, as silly as he might be. And the *duc* who wanted to give you *carte blanche*."

"Oh, them! I never felt the least bit tempted to confide in them. To be intimate with them."

"As you do with Nicholas."

"I may be. Yes. But—"

"But what?"

"But if I give in to my feelings, will he turn on me? Betray me, as Peter did? Are all men like Peter?"

"I see." Georgina chewed thoughtfully on her thumbnail. "Dear, it is quite understandable that you should feel this way, that you should be so wary of giving your trust again. Peter treated you shockingly. I knew he was a bad 'un, even when we were at school. It is a miracle you can even think of being close to another man."

"Yes! That is just what I fear."

"Well, Lizzie, let me assure you that not all men are like Peter Everdean. They are out there, oh yes, and you must be careful of them. Like my second husband, Sir Everett."

The two women shuddered in concert. The late,

unlamented Sir Everett had been quite wealthy, but very stingy. He had also been quite fat and quite temperamental. He had bred yappy French poodles on his country estate, and Georgina had often been compelled to tend their kennels.

"You must always avoid men who wear corsets and gorge themselves on fig pudding, at all costs," Georgina now admonished. "I would never have looked twice at him, if I hadn't been so desperate when Jack died. And then, you see, there are men like Jack."

The friends sighed in remembrance. Captain Jack Reid had been tall, blond, charming, dashing in his regimentals. He had been a younger son with few prospects, but all the girls at Miss Thompson's had been quite in love with him. Georgina, older than Elizabeth and quite dashing herself, had been the envy of the school when she had eloped with him to Gretna Green and then gone with him to Portugal. He had been killed there in battle.

"Oh, Lizzie," Georgina said. "Our rough months in those drafty billets were perfect."

"Jack was handsome," Elizabeth answered.

"And as good as he was handsome." Georgina twisted on her wrist the narrow pearl bracelet he had given her, which never left her person. "He was not the most intellectual man, true, but he loved that I wanted to be an artist."

"What of Mr. Beaumont?"

"Ah, well, Lizzie, you needn't fear that Nicholas will be another Mr. Beaumont." Aloysius Beaumont, wealthy cit, had been all of seventy-six when he had married Georgina, and seventy-seven when she buried him. He had been elderly, but generous.

"And rather nice, when he could recall who I was,"

Georgina said. "And if it were not for him, we could never have had the things we do on the pittance Sir Everett's children allow me."

"And what a shame that would have been! Every grocer and dressmaker in Italy would be destitute," Elizabeth teased.

"So, my dear, perhaps you should take a chance with Nicholas. You need not tell him quite everything, even if you are lovers. He may turn out to be your Jack. Or at least an amusement."

Elizabeth hugged Georgina, but in her heart, she was screaming, *but what if he does not want to be my Jack?*

9

"YOU ARE VERY LATE."

Nicholas paused at the sound of Elizabeth's voice, still poised over the candle he was lighting. Slowly, he turned to look at her.

Elizabeth sat, very still and pale, in the comer of the dark foyer, hands folded in her lap as she watched him. She was dressed for a party, in sky-blue muslin trimmed in white satin ribbon, her hair plaited and caught up in ivory combs. She looked like the Parmigianino Madonna, all slender neck and mysterious, downcast eyes.

"I thought perhaps you had had a contretemps with an irate client," she continued, coming to take the flint from his frozen fingers and lighting the candle herself. "You are not one to forget a party."

He slapped his open palm against his forehead. "The Vincenzis' party! I was to escort you. I am sorry, Elizabeth. I was just walking. I lost track of the time."

"That is quite all right. As it is raining, we can't go out into their lovely gardens anyway. Everyone will be smothering in their tiny ballroom. Georgina has gone ahead." She smiled up at him, her mouth turning suddenly down as she saw his hair dripping onto the carpet. "You must be frozen through! Come into the kitchen where there is a fire, before you catch the ague."

Nicholas allowed her to lead him into the warm kitchen, and fuss over him with towels and warm kettles. But he, who had never had a modest day from the time he could toddle away from his nurse and pull off his nappy, balked when she asked him to remove his shirt.

"Wh-what?" he stammered.

"I said you should remove your shirt," Elizabeth answered calmly, stirring at the brewing tea. "It is soaked through."

"I am not certain that is a very good idea."

Elizabeth laughed. "Oh, please, Nicholas! Do not go missish now. Your teeth are chattering, and if you make yourself ill, I will not see a farthing of payment for a month." She slanted him a sly smile. "I already saw a great deal on the terrace last night, you know. I promise to use my artistic detachment and refrain from ravishing you here in my kitchen."

Nicholas couldn't help but laugh at himself. He was behaving rather like a spinster aunt, shivering in wet clothes in order to preserve a doubtful modesty. This, after all, was a woman he had held, kissed, planned to kidnap. He pulled off the sodden shirt and leaned back in his chair, relishing the heat of the fire and the cozy sounds of Elizabeth's tuneless humming and the soft patter of the rain.

"Here we are!" Elizabeth arranged the tea service on a small table, and sat beside him to pour. "A nice pot of tea, some brandy if you need something a bit stronger, and even some sandwiches Bianca had put away in the pantry."

"It looks lovely," Nicholas answered, gratefully accepting the liberally laced cup of tea she offered. "But I do not want you to waste your evening waiting on me. You should be at the party."

Elizabeth waved away his protest. "Not at all. This is ever so much nicer than yet another party. I'm quite enjoying the quiet. And the company."

"So you tire of the social whirl?"

"A bit. I love the gatherings. Venice is a delight, and there are so many artists here." She paused to take a thoughtful bite of sandwich. "But at times it can be rather overwhelming, and I forget the perfect pleasures of a good fire on a rainy night."

"Carnivale will soon be over."

"Yes."

"What will you do then? Stay and watch Venice in its Lenten solemnities?"

"Settle down to my work, you mean?" Elizabeth chuckled. "Yes, I do need to do that. The Bruni commission will not wait forever, and I have a few things I am working on for myself. Georgie has suggested we take a villa in the country for Lent, somewhere nearer Venice than her home at Lake Como."

"Do you approve of this plan?" He listened to her carefully, straining for a glimpse of wistfulness, longing for a return to English aristocratic country life. If she could be persuaded to return on her own...

"Oh, yes. The country would be very conducive to my work."

"So you do tire of city life?"

"Not a bit!" She poured herself another cup of tea. "I am having a wonderful time here. So many patrons eager to spend their money! And we must come back here in the spring, anyway."

"Return? Why so?"

"I received a letter this afternoon, a new commission. To restore the Veronese frescoes in Lady Deake's Ca Donati. I am to begin work on them in April, when Lady Deake returns from Rome."

"What?" Nicholas almost fell from his chair in his shock. "Lady Evelyn Deake—you will be working for her?"

"Yes." Elizabeth frowned. "Nicholas, whatever is the matter? This a perfect commission—every artist in Venice has been vying for it. It is a great honor to be so singled out, even by someone as thoroughly irritating as Lady Deake."

"Elizabeth." Nicholas knelt before her, her hands between his. If Elizabeth spoke with Evelyn, if Evelyn told her who he truly was. all would be lost. "Listen to me. You have traveled all over Italy. You have seen so much."

"Yes, that is true." Her voice was puzzled, her forehead creased in concern as she looked down at him. She obviously thought him moon-mad.

Still he plunged on, hardly knowing or caring that he was babbling. "Perhaps it is time you expanded your experience, discovered a new culture."

"A new culture? Such as France?"

"Perhaps. Or even England."

She snatched her hands from his. "England!"

"There are many fine artists there."

"Absolutely not! There is nothing to be learned there. This is my home, and here I will stay." She took a long sip from the brandy bottle, sitting there marble-still, eyes closed, until she visibly composed herself. "Oh, Nicholas, do sit down. What is wrong with you tonight? First you walk about in the rain, and now you are full of England for some reason."

Nicholas reluctantly sat back in his chair, watching her, the glitter of her eyes as she suppressed tears, the mulish set of her dainty jaw. Never had he known such desperation before. He had thought himself quite prepared to do anything to take her back to England and Peter, and then go on with his life. Now he trembled with something very like fear that she would discover the truth from Evelyn's painted lips, that her laughter and kisses would be lost forever when she knew.

As they would when she was kidnapped by himself and the nasty Benno.

He did not want that, he saw now. He only wanted to go on like this always, sitting beside her in a firelit kitchen with the rain whispering at the windows.

"There is no reason," he said, smiling at her in reassurance. "No reason at all."

ELIZABETH LAY awake for long hours that night, watching the silvery fall of rain outside her window and thinking of Nicholas's words that evening.

She knew him so little. For all his charm, his dimpled grins, his wondrous kisses, he was yet a stranger. She knew nothing of his motives, his past. She had not wanted to ask, for fear of opening the Pandora's Box of her own past. And he was such fun, so good at his job, that it had not seemed all that important.

Until now. Now, when he had shown her such seriousness, such barely veiled desperation. She had never thought to see that in his merry countenance. He had been so earnest when he urged her to give up

Lady Deake's patronage and return to England. His intensity as he had gripped her hands had been almost frightening.

Could he truly miss England so much himself that he hoped his employment with her would take him back there? That seemed so flimsy an excuse. She would not have thought him such a patriot as all that. In her speculations on his past, she had supposed him to be fleeing England like herself, in search of adventure and fortune. Or perhaps fleeing a broken heart

"Of course!" Elizabeth whispered to herself. "It was the mention of Lady Deake that brought on this rage to leave Venice."

They had been conversing so closely at the opera. Elizabeth shuddered at the memory of Lady Deake's bright curls nodding near Nicholas's shoulder as she giggled up at him.

Lady Deake must have been a part of his past, or had at least known him before. And if he had been moving in such a smart set as that, he was not the middle-class soldier she had supposed him to be. What a coil!

He had been living under their roof, eating his meals across the table from her, watching her paint, teasing Bianca, bantering with Georgina. He was not intrusive, did not at all mind their erratic ways, and was very good at his job, willing to deal with very unpleasant people to collect what was owed to her. In his short tenure, he had persuaded no fewer than three clients to pay their accounts in full, leaving only two particularly stubborn ones in arrears. Elizabeth had bought a dashing new blue velvet cloak, paid Georgina her share of the rent, and still had coin left over.

But more than that, clients now looked at her with

a different air, a respectful air, a professional air. There were no more lewd remarks, no more agreeing on one price then paying another when the work was complete. It was quite marvelous.

And entirely due to Nicholas. In their household, he was charming, witty, a little silly, a little roguish. In public, he was every bit a commanding military man, stern and uncompromising with all who owed her money. The hard glint in his onyx eyes could even make Elizabeth stand up straighter.

Yet he never spoke of himself. Georgina was an unrepentant snoop, with a positive gift for ferreting out people's secrets whether they wished her to or not. All her leading questions over the breakfast table only earned a grin, a "That is far too dull a topic to discuss over these superb scones," and perhaps a suggestive comment concerning one of her late husbands.

Elizabeth's more delicate inquiries had fared no better. Their conversations were always interesting; he was a very intelligent man, and witty as well. But they always concerned business, Italian art, or gossip about the people they met at social gatherings. He never inquired about her own past, except for that night on the terrace; he never spoke of his own.

"I will find out the truth." Elizabeth climbed out of bed and lit a candle, searching through her cluttered writing table for a sheet of notepaper. "I will simply write and ask Lady Deake to tea, before she leaves for Rome."

10

"HE HAS SETTLED WELL INTO secretarydom." Georgina paused in sipping cognac and sketching in her book to glance at Nicholas, who had crossed the crowded terrace at Florian's Cafe to speak to one of Elizabeth's clients who was in arrears.

Elizabeth popped a small tea cake into her mouth and chewed absently, watching with avid interest as Nicholas's gleaming white grin flashed in the sunlight. He really was an utterly handsome specimen of manhood, despite his odd behavior.

Yes, gorgeous but mysterious.

Elizabeth was, in fact, becoming utterly and dizzily obsessed with her secretive secretary who kissed like an angel. She was becoming like a schoolgirl mooning over the dancing master. It was completely ridiculous, but there it was.

She was blushing fire red just thinking about it; she could feel the color creeping down her throat. Nicholas looked up then, caught her staring at him with cake crumbs on her chin, and grinned his wonderful, infuriating grin.

"Oh!" She groaned, snatching up her napkin and scrubbing furiously at the crumbs.

"Blast it all, Lizzie, just bed him and get it over with!" Georgina muttered. Her gloved hand reached out for another of the cakes.

"If only I could." Then she would know what it was like, would know what Nicholas looked like with no clothes at all, and she could then go on with her life.

Perhaps.

"Why can you not?"

"You know perfectly well why, Georgie."

Georgina shook her head hard enough to set the feathers on her bonnet bobbing. "Tell me, dear."

"I ought not to get so very close to someone, particularly an Englishman. He may know someone who knew me in Derbyshire."

"What does one thing have to do with the other? He won't necessarily guess your secrets simply because he sees you in your chemise."

"Georgie! Some women may be able to take a lover and not spill all their secrets at once, but I could not. I would feel I had to tell him all, silly me."

Georgina nodded. "You do have rather a revealing face."

"I already feel horrible about deceiving him so. And he is only the secretary now." The secretary she kissed passionately.

"Lizzie, you are making far too much of this! You must simply steel yourself and keep silent. And if you talked too much, you would not have enough time for the amusing bits, anyway. That is what an affair is for, after all."

The amusing bits. That sounded rather promising. Still, Elizabeth shook her head. "I wish I could feel as you do. It would make things so much simpler.

"But Nicholas would have to know he was bedding a murderess."

"Shh!" Georgina squeezed her hand, her forehead creased in a fierce frown. "I told you never to use that word, Lizzie. It is utterly untrue. You were merely defending yourself against a monster. And when I think of it, I could go and murder that stepbrother of yours myself for putting you through that!"

"Georgie "

"No! What occurred was entirely his fault, not yours. You deserve happiness, Lizzie. But that is not all that is keeping you from Nicholas, is it, dear?"

Elizabeth bit her lip and glanced away. "No. I think..."

"Nicholas!" Georgina looked up with a too-bright smile as Nicholas appeared beside them. "We were just speaking of you. Care for some cognac?"

"Thank you, Georgina, cognac sounds perfect. And I hope you were only saying very interesting things about me."

"Georgie only ever says interesting things," Elizabeth commented. "Particularly about handsome men."

Georgina rolled her eyes. "I was only remarking on what a consummate businessman you are, Nicholas. Exactly what Lizzie needed."

Nicholas laughed, his head tipped back to reveal the strength of his tanned throat above his snowy cravat. "I certainly hope that may be the case, madam."

Elizabeth smiled reluctantly. It was always thus when he was about; no matter what her fears or worries, he could make her laugh or smile. Simply by his presence. "Absolutely."

"Then perhaps this will help solidify my position." He tossed a small velvet pouch into Elizabeth's lap. She opened it, and gold spilled onto her palm. Enough, more than enough, for a daring blue silk gown she had coveted in a dressmaker's window.

The gown she had hoped could entice Nicholas into another indiscretion. "What?"

"The last of what Signor Visconti owes you for that sketch of his children. He just paid me."

"That stubborn old goat?" Elizabeth squealed with joy, and leaned forward to kiss Nicholas's cheek in impromptu thanksgiving. "You are a wonder, Nicholas!"

His arm tightened around her waist, clinging. Elizabeth drew back a little to look up at him, puzzled. He was watching her, his eyes narrow and opaque, no hint of his rakish smile. He stared at her as if he had never seen her before, and had not the least notion of how she had come to be half on his lap.

Perhaps he was not so unaffected by their kiss as he had seemed. Tentatively, Elizabeth reached out her thumb to wipe away the trace of tinted lip salve she had left on his cheek. His jaw tightened, but he did not move away. Instead, he leaned, just barely, into her hand. His silken curls brushed against her fingers.

It was the most intimate moment Elizabeth had ever known, and it was over in an instant. Like the sun crawling from the clouds, Nicholas laughed, pressed a hasty kiss into her palm, and deposited her firmly back into her own chair.

If not for the lingering warmth on her hand, she could have said she imagined the whole incident. Nicholas's brief intensity was gone, and he was laughing with Georgina.

Elizabeth forced a smile to her own lips, and ducked her head over her open sketchbook.

"Well, *mes amis*, I must be away!" Georgina gathered her sketches, her parasol, and her reticule, and rose to her feet in a rustle of butter-yellow silk skirts. "I have a new model I am interviewing for my scene of Apollo and Daphne."

"Not another Paolo!" Elizabeth cried. More than one handsome model, lovestruck for Georgina, had turned their houses head-over-ears with midnight serenades, lavish bouquets that blocked the corridors, and even, on one memorable occasion, a gift of a squealing piglet. Elizabeth had quite enjoyed the respite from models.

"Certainly not, Lizzie! I am through utterly with Paolos." Georgina kissed Elizabeth's cheek, then, giggling, Nicholas's. "I will see you tonight. Do not forget our theater engagement, my dears, it's *The Merchant of Venice*!"

With a twinkle of her fingers, she was gone, leaving Elizabeth quite alone with Nicholas. If one considered a table in the most crowded cafe in Venice quite alone. To Elizabeth, it felt as if it were.

Nicholas helped himself to the last cake. "And what are you going to do with this fine afternoon, Elizabeth? No models to inspect?"

Elizabeth laughed. "Not a one, I fear! No sittings, either, since Signora Bruni canceled. I was thinking of taking a tour of Santi Giovanni in Brogana," she said, mentioning the fifteenth-century church she had often seen but never gone inside.

"Why that? Sounds dusty."

"Because, pagan, an artist should never pass up an opportunity to observe a church or palace. It may prove most edifying. Or at least something to do of an afternoon, while waiting for the night's festivities to begin!"

"Hmm, well, in that case, Madame Artiste, I shall accompany you. You have quite convinced me of the charms of old churches. And you need an escort."

An unwilling little thrill made Elizabeth's heart beat just a tiny bit faster. An entire afternoon, alone with him! "Well," she said, a teasing reluctance in her voice, "if you feel it would be quite dangerous for me to venture to the church alone..."

"Oh yes, it is. One never knows about those vicious nuns. And you could educate me on the finer points of Gothic architecture."

"You could not be such an infidel if you know that Santi Giovanni is in the Gothic style. There is an intellectual hiding inside of you, Nicholas."

"You have found me out again!" He drank the very last of the cognac, and smiled at her. "I must send off a quick message, and then we can be on our way."

Elizabeth smiled and nodded, telling herself that the strain in his voice, the light in his dark eyes, was surely all in her imagination. He was quite her merry Nicholas again.

"...DOMED and columned in the Gothic style. It was once the funeral church of the doges, including..."

Elizabeth leaned against Nicholas's shoulder with a suppressed sigh. An historical outing had seemed such a good idea. Churches usually fascinated her, and Santi Giovanni in Brogana was quite magnificent. But somehow the warmth of the incense and the beeswax candles, along with the droning voice of the guide, and the cakes and cognac she had consumed at Florian's, were conspiring to put her to sleep where she stood.

"You are not attending," Nicholas whispered. "Should you not be writing all of this down?"

"Shh," she answered. "I am contemplating."

"You are drowsing. Come, I have a much better idea for our afternoon."

Elizabeth brightened a bit. "What?"

"Come along, and I will show you."

"But the tour is not finished!"

"We will just slip around that candelabra, see, and out that door, and be gone in a trice. That old tour guide will never even notice."

"But where?"

"Just come with me! You will not regret it, Elizabeth, I swear."

So she went.

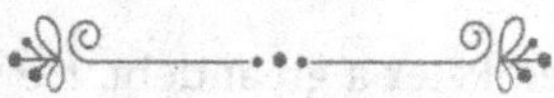

He could not do it.

Nicholas took Elizabeth as far as the secluded canal where an empty boat was waiting, only to find that he could not possibly force her into it and take her away. It was not just because of their passionate interlude on the terrace. He could not put fear and disillusionment into the silver-gray eyes that were laughing up at him now.

He had done horrible, terrible things in his life, but this he could not. Elizabeth quite simply deserved better than to be hauled off summarily like a bundle of freight, like a possession. She deserved—

Well, what she truly deserved was to be left to live her life in peace, to be allowed to have her career and make her choices with no interference. It was a realization that quite startled Nicholas. He had always liked women, of course, but he had always put them into tidy compartments in his life. There were young things in white muslin at Almack's who were not to be touched, and courtesans and daring widows who were safe to trifle with. And then, in a compartment all her own, was his mother.

This was a new way of seeing the world, to consider that a woman was a person, with thoughts and talents and wishes all her own, and a right to make choices.

It had taken extraordinary women, like his wonderful Elizabeth and her outrageous, independent "sister," to make him realize this. And yet it was too late.

He still owed Peter a great debt. He was still obligated to take Elizabeth back to England, by some means. But not this way. Not by force and fear.

He would simply have to think of something else.

"Well?" Elizabeth said, tapping her half boot impatiently and interrupting his moment of epiphany. "What are we going to do?"

He had to think quickly. What did ladies like to do? "Shop!"

"What?"

"Shop. On the Rialto."

"Oh!" Elizabeth laughed, obviously thinking of the bright new coins in her reticule that were simply burning to be spent. "What a grand idea! And what a unique gentleman you are, Nicholas, to think an afternoon of shopping would be all the crack."

"Oh, my dear." Nicholas half turned her, so she

would not see him wave off the lurking Benno. "You do not know the half of what I think the 'crack' is."

LATER THAT EVENING, when he had deposited Elizabeth at the house with her new purchases so she could dress for the night's festivities, Nicholas drifted aimlessly through the narrow walkways of Venice. He was quite unmindful of the light rain that had begun to fall and that soaked his bare head and dripped onto the collar of his greatcoat. He didn't heed the passersby who knocked into him and hurried on, or the beggar children who sometimes appeared underfoot. He did not see the buildings, some magnificent. and some squalid, or the piles of refuse and the lines of sodden laundry.

He could only see Elizabeth.

Never in his life had Nicholas Hollingsworth, war hero, dedicated rogue, and nobleman's bastard, felt so completely out of sorts. Even in battle he had had a sword and pistol to defend himself. Yet before a pair of quiet gray eyes he was utterly defenseless. What little was left of his honor was vulnerable to her smile.

He had paid off a very irate Benno, who had not been at all happy that his carefully planned trap had come to naught. Nicholas had sent the odious little man away, and now he was left with no plan at all. No ideas for taking Elizabeth to England and into the care of her stepbrother.

He could only now admit that he did not want to take her to England. And for one very selfish reason. He was happy. Truly happy.

Nicholas loved living in the narrow house on the canal. He loved breakfasting with Elizabeth and Georgina, sharing the English newspapers with them, and listening to their laughter and their plans. He loved the smells of turpentine and chalk that floated down the corridors, watching a blank canvas come to a true and sparkling life under Elizabeth's brush. He loved dancing with her at a ball, or just watching her across a room as she talked with her friends, her elflike face alive with enthusiasm. And yes, he even loved to spar with that ridiculous Sir Stephen, who still imagined he might have a chance with Elizabeth. "This is horrendous." He groaned and leaned back against a damp wall. "Of all times for me to become disgustingly content. Of all places! Of all women."

Nicholas closed his eyes.

Peter had been the best friend Nicholas had ever known, until he found Elizabeth. Peter had not always been so cold, so unbending. He had lived with Nicholas through the terrors of war, the deaths of comrades, and the deadly dull times of waiting in dusty Spanish billets. He had saved Nicholas's life, not just on that battlefield, but numerous times, with his company.

Yes, Nicholas was happy in Elizabeth's company. He could stay for eternity in that chaotic house and never want to leave. Surely he owed the woman he could love a happy life, a life of her own choosing. And, for whatever reason, she very clearly chose not to live that life with her stepbrother. There were secrets in her life, he knew. His honor told him that he owed it to Peter to keep his word.

Nicholas opened his eyes and stared up at the slate-colored heavens, letting the rains pour down over his face.

"Tell me what to do!" he shouted. "Tell me what is right."

It was the closest he had ever come to a prayer.

11

LONDON

"WHAT IS WRONG, *MON CHER*?"

Peter Everdean, Earl of Clifton, turned from the fire to glance at the woman who reclined in his bed. Her hair spilled sun gold over the brocade sheets and her fetching white shoulders, but he was unmoved. Detached.

"Go back to sleep, Yvette," he murmured.

"But, *mon cher*!" She pouted prettily, stretching against the pillows. "Eet ees very lonely here in this huge bed, and I cannot sleep when I am lonely."

"Yvette!" He slapped his palm against the arm of his chair, startling awake the greyhound that slept by the hearth. "I said go back to sleep. I am trying to think, and your egregious false French accent is not helping matters."

Yvette slid beneath the bedclothes, wide-eyed, and Peter returned to his absent contemplation of the red-orange flames.

He had thought, hoped, that bringing the oh-so-talented Yvette to his London town house would help him to forget, if only for an hour or two. It had not. Even her soft moans, her practiced sighs as she moved beneath him, had not erased Elizabeth from his worries.

Where was she, by Jove? It had been weeks since Nick Hollingsworth had gone to Italy, and there had not been a single message from him. Not a word as to whether she had been located, what she was doing, if she was well or ill.

He had to see her again, to see that she was alive. To bury his head in her cool hands and beg her forgiveness for his monstrous behavior. He had been insane when he came home from the Peninsula, tormented by memories and nightmares, by the ever-present sound of gunfire in his ears. By what he had lost.

During the years he had been gone, fighting, Elizabeth had represented all that was good about life and home. Her girlish, long-awaited letters, scented with lilies of the valley, had meant Clifton Manor to him, home and safety and quiet.

After Spain, after Carmen, he had wanted only the green sweetness of home, the sound of his sister's laughter.

He had somehow thought she could make him whole and pure again, but instead he had come back to England to find that she looked so Spanish. So like Carmen. And she had not been the sweet girl of his memory; she had been independent, defiant. He had been overcome by the crazy thought that she was Carmen, that she was there to torment him.

But now she was gone, and he had spent two long years resting, recovering, and most of all regretting what had passed between them.

"Oh, Lizzie," he whispered. "How can I ever make you understand if you are not here? How can I make you see the truth?" He, who had always sworn to protect her, had driven her to murder and life in exile. Elizabeth, his sister, whom he had taught to ride a pony and danced with at country assemblies. His dear, talented Lizzie. He had driven her away.

He wanted so much to tell her the truth, to restore the easy affection, the trust that had been between them so long ago.

It was becoming increasingly obvious that Nicholas, the greatest hope he had had in these two years, was not about his job properly.

Peter would simply have to travel to Italy himself.

"I WAS SO VERY happy to receive your note, Miss Cheswood!" Lady Deake practically glowed with sweetness and light as she welcomed Elizabeth into the vast marble foyer of her Ca Donati. "I do so want to become better acquainted with you."

Elizabeth somehow doubted that. She was a mere hired artist, a servant. Surely not someone Lady Deake would wish to be bosom bows with. But Evelyn's artificial amity suited Elizabeth's purposes very well indeed, so she allowed her arm to be taken as Evelyn led her into a sumptuous green-and-gold morning room.

"I am happy it was not an inconvenient time to view your frescoes, Lady Deake," Elizabeth said, as she seated herself on a satin slipper chair by the fire and arranged the pink skirts of her walking dress.

"Not at all, not at all. Venice is so very dead in the afternoon. No teas or card parties at all." With an airy wave of her diamond-bedecked hand, Evelyn dismissed the crowded canal of afternoon revelers outside her window. "Before I show you the ever-so-adorable paintings, we must have some tea."

Elizabeth opened her mouth to reply, but Evelyn quickly interrupted.

"No, I insist! I get so few chances to talk with another Englishwoman these days."

Elizabeth watched as Evelyn fussed with a gilt tea service, and speculated on exactly how to bring the conversation about to the topic of Nicholas. She did not want to arouse Lady Deake's suspicions, after all. Finally she said, "You must miss your life in England very much, Lady Deake."

Evelyn sighed dramatically. "Oh, indeed! I have a great many friends in London, and they are ever so much more agreeable than most of the people I have encountered here thus far. But then, London is quite dull at this time of year, and I absolutely abhor the country. So I decided to come abroad. So stylish now, to be on the Continent. And Italy does have its charms."

"To be sure," Elizabeth agreed.

"Has it been very long since you were in England, Miss Cheswood?"

Not long enough, Elizabeth thought. "Oh, yes. I hardly remember it. Yet I feel I know it very well. My new secretary has such vivid stories of English life."

"Ah, yes. The beauteous Nicholas. He would have fascinating things to tell, I'm sure." Evelyn's smile had turned distinctly feline.

Elizabeth nodded calmly and sipped her tea, concealing her anticipation behind a conspiratorial giggle. Lady Deake must surely have known Nicholas before! "Were you possibly acquainted with Mr. Carter in England, Lady Deake?"

"With Mr. Carter?" Evelyn visibly started, as if she had suddenly recalled something, and she stared down into her cup. "No, no. I have never seen him before the night at the opera, ever. He is just... I am just... well, I am rather a connoisseur, you know. Of handsome gentlemen. Like your Mr. Carter." Evelyn laughed nervously. "Would you care for more tea, Miss Cheswood?"

"Yes, thank you." Elizabeth watched Evelyn with a thoughtful frown. Something was definitely in the air. Lady Deake was a very silly woman, but she was a very poor liar. She had known Nicholas before that night at the opera, it was quite obvious. It was also obvious that she was concealing something very interesting indeed.

"Perhaps, Lady Deake, you could show me the Veronese now?" Elizabeth said, with her warmest smile.

He was going to have to tell her. Yes. This very moment, he would go to her and tell her the truth, before she could hear it from the mouth of someone like Lady Deake.

Elizabeth would very likely hate him. She would

cast him out of her life, out of her golden circle. But perhaps, just perhaps, she would first listen to him, and would come to understand at least a bit of what he was about.

Perhaps she would even consider agreeing to see Peter again.

But perhaps he should wait just one day more, until Carnivale was over. Then he would have one last ball at her side, a time to dance with her and be next to her. Nicholas groaned and rolled over on his narrow bed, lying on his bare stomach to watch the shadows lengthen across the floor. His dilemma seemed perpetual, never-ending. Peter and his promise stood for the honor that was all that he could truly call his own. Elizabeth was all the things he had scoffed at, claimed could not exist—things such as pure talent and unselfish friendship.

Growing up in his mother's house, cold and dark, and then at a succession of schools noted for their strict modes of discipline, his life had been distinctly devoid of such things as laughter and art. He had always been in the shadow of his father, the illustrious Duke of Ainsley, who was forever attempting to control his bastard son's life, despite his abandonment of that son's mother so long ago.

Nicholas had suffered under his father's dictates, under the scorn of his stepmother and his proper half-sisters, until he had gone to war to escape them, and to escape himself.

In Spain he had found a certain rough camaraderie, a shallow sort of friendship based on shared danger and determined debauchery. It had been different with Peter Everdean. They had talked together a great deal, of hopes for the future, memories of England, and of women. Yet Peter had never been much for laughter, except for the brief reign in his life of a dark-eyed senorita named Carmen.

It had taken Elizabeth to bring Nicholas all he had missed in life. She gave freely of her affection, her laughter; she had let him into the charmed circle of her life. She never asked about his past, his fortune and connections.

She was concerned only with him.

He would tell her the truth. She deserved that. Tonight. Or perhaps tomorrow morning

A COUNTRY VILLA!

Elizabeth stared down at Georgina's hastily scrawled note, sent off from an estate agent's office before she dashed away to a sitting. A country villa, dreaming in the sun, sounded like Paradise after the social wildness of the past weeks. She could truly work there, complete the Bruni commission, and the sketches of Nicholas she had been working on secretly late at night. Rather naughty sketches, if she did say so herself, of a heavy-eyed Nicholas, half dressed, and clearly in love.

She giggled then at her own folly, and fell back onto the bed without even removing her bonnet or shoes. She watched the patterns of the sun move lazily across the ceiling.

Of *course* he was not in love with her! As much as

she did wish it, with a force that almost frightened her, men as handsome as Greek gods did not fall in love with small, dark women with paint beneath their fingernails.

No, they fell in love with blond, angelic, proper misses, who painted polite watercolors and never, ever drank too much champagne at balls. Nicholas might laugh and even flirt with her, but then he laughed and flirted with everyone. Even Georgina and Bianca, and Katerina Bruni, who flashed her green eyes at him during sittings.

Elizabeth sighed and rolled over, reaching beneath the mattress to retrieve the sketches that were hidden there. She leafed through them, smiling. He was lovely, especially when he smiled at her, his head bent toward hers as they spoke together. It was very difficult to remember why she had sworn off men when she was near him—he melted away the walls of ice around her soul when he smiled.

He was not like any man she had ever known. He was intelligent, though he tried so hard to hide it behind silly grins, and he respected intelligence in her. He listened to her, appreciated what she was trying to do with her work.

And he was a divine kisser. Absolutely top of the trees!

Once, frightened and cold, she had vowed never to believe what any man said to her. Yet here she was, beginning to trust, to love a man as dashing and mysterious as Nicholas.

Perhaps in the country, far away from the distractions of sittings and social gatherings, she would discover the true man behind Nicholas's façade. She would draw him out, about the past and the future.

Perhaps she could even tell him a little, a very little, of her own life.

Filled with the rosy glow of hope, Elizabeth pushed the sketches back into their hiding place, and went to tell Nicholas of their travel plans.

12

"CAN YOU SEE IT yet, Lizzie? What is it like?"

Elizabeth leaned further out of the carriage window, one gloved hand clapped firmly onto her bonnet to prevent it from flying away. "I cannot see it yet, Georgie," she called back over her shoulder.

"Well, what do you see?"

Elizabeth looked about her. The narrow road they were traveling hugged a precarious cliff that looked out over an impossibly blue sea. White breakers crashed and roiled on the rocks below.

"Only sea," she answered. "Oh, it is glorious! It's as if we were flying above the water on bird's wings. You should look, Georgie!"

Georgina waved a handkerchief in front of her green-tinged face. "No, I thank you! It is certainly bad enough to be riding in here without seeing what is outside. Can the driver not go slower?"

"You asked him to hurry." Elizabeth sat back in the carriage, and pushed the tendrils of loose hair back beneath her bonnet. "Perhaps some fresh air is what you require, Georgie. If you would lean your head out of the window—"

"No! I shall be well by the time we arrive, I vow. Perhaps some cool water would help, though."

"Let me get it for you." Elizabeth pulled their hamper from beneath her seat and rummaged about for the flask of water and a cup. Poor Georgina, it was ever thus when they traveled, she reflected. It seemed her friend's only weakness.

Georgina gratefully accepted the water and sipped at it carefully. Soon her color seemed a bit more pink than green. She even smiled a little. "I am glad Nicholas has gone ahead to be certain the villa has been properly aired. I vow I shall go directly to bed, and eat only custard and clear broth for a week."

"We are supposed to do some work at least, Georgie, while we are here."

"Oh, yes, yes. Work. There will be more than enough time for that, with no balls or routs to attend. But I daresay we will have some fun."

"No models, I beg of you!"

"Certainly not! Nicholas will be the only man we will see. And as I am sure you will not share him, the rest of us will be quite nun-like." Georgina sighed dramatically.

Elizabeth laughed. "He is not mine to share!"

"Is he not? Then why were you such a mooncalf these three days he has been gone?"

"I was not! I have been far too occupied in packing our trunks to concern myself overmuch with his absence."

"Um-hm." Georgina just smiled. "Would you hand me those biscuits, dear? You have so diverted me that I no longer feel even a twinge of illness."

Elizabeth passed Georgina the tin of biscuits, hoping for silence. It was not to be.

Georgina nibbled a bit at the biscuit; even her eyes

seemed to sparkle now with some of her usual vitality. "You have missed him, have you not, Lizzie? Just a bit?"

"Perhaps, just a bit," Elizabeth replied, with a small sigh. "Venice seemed so very much quieter without him there."

"Hmm. That may be due in a very small way to the fact that Carnivale is at an end, and we have had no parties to go to."

"That is only a small part of it!" Elizabeth laughed. "Our own house has been quieter, as well. It is nice to have someone about to give a male opinion every once in a while. Yes, I missed him."

"Lizzie." Georgina frowned a bit, suddenly serious. She reached out and touched Elizabeth's hand. "Are you in love with Nicholas?"

Elizabeth laughed again, nervously. She drew her hand away, and patted at a strand of hair that had strayed to her neck. "Love? Oh, Georgie, what a thing to ask!"

"Yes, I know. Are you?"

"I hardly know. I have only known him a few weeks."

"Sometimes only a few hours will suffice," Georgina murmured. "I know you are fond of him; that is obvious. But are your feelings deeper than that, dear?"

Elizabeth stared down at her folded hands for a long moment, a realization slowly growing in her mind. She could scarce admit it, even to herself, but "Yes. I suppose I am falling in love with Nicholas."

"Oh." Georgina turned to look out of the window.

"Georgie, what is it?" Elizabeth cried. "You like Nicholas, do you not? You have urged me to spend time with him."

"Yes, dear, I have, and I do not feel I have been

wrong in that. I feel he is a good man, as well as a handsome and charming one."

"Then what is wrong?" Elizabeth caught her lower lip between her teeth. "Is it that you fear he does not return my regard?"

"No, Lizzie! Quite the opposite. But I sense—" Georgina paused.

"What?"

"I sense that Nicholas, for all his virtues, is not all that he appears to be."

"Whatever do you mean, not what he appears to be?" A growing panic seemed to climb from Elizabeth's stomach to her throat. "Have you heard something concerning him?"

"No, Lizzie! It is only a sense. I cannot explain it, it is simply a feeling."

"You think I am foolish to have this regard for him?"

"Not at all. I am merely saying be cautious. I know I told you to follow your heart, dear, and so you should, but at the same time do not let your love blind you completely." Georgina took Elizabeth's hands again, and smiled reassuringly. "I have a great deal more experience with men than you, for good or ill. I like Nicholas, truly, but I must advise you now not to be too rash, Lizzie. Yes?"

Elizabeth squeezed her friend's hands in return. "Yes. I will do as you advise."

"Very good! And remember—one can be cautious and still be merry. This time is for you to rest, to think, to be comfortable with people who care about you. Such as me—and Nicholas."

"Oh, Georgie!" Elizabeth kissed Georgina's cheek. "I am the most fortunate woman in the world to have a friend such as you."

"Not half as fortunate as I, dear Lizzie." Georgina held her close for an instant, then sat back with a smile. "And now, I think I will just rest a moment, before we reach the villa."

Elizabeth nodded and returned to her contemplation of the landscape. "We will be isolated here. I have not seen a structure, a person, or even a goat for fully half an hour."

Yet even as she spoke the road turned and they faced a downward slope into a wide green valley. Tiny cottages and a large, medieval church were laid out below like a toy village. They seemed to sparkle in the afternoon sunlight, a fairy kingdom.

And set above the storybook hamlet on a verdant hillside was a villa, its white stucco and red-tile roof softened by climbing ivy and pots of red and pink flowers lined up on the terrace.

A man was waiting on that terrace for their arrival, his black hair undulating like a satin ribbon in the light breeze.

Elizabeth leaned out of the window again when she saw him, and waved madly.

"Oh, Georgie!" she cried. "It is beautiful! It is going to be such a wonderful month."

When the carriage drew to a halt, Nicholas was there to open the door and help them down.

His hands lingered warmly for just a moment longer than was proper on Elizabeth's waist. "Welcome to your new home," he said, and kissed her cheek. "I hope you will like it. I filled every room with flowers, just for you."

"Then I am sure I shall." And over his shoulder, she smiled at Georgina. All would be well after all.

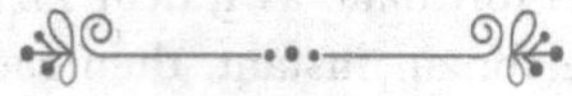

"IF YOU DO NOT STOP FIDGETING, Nicholas, I will not be able to finish before the light changes!" Elizabeth waved her paintbrush at Nicholas, and stamped her bare foot on the grass.

Nicholas settled back into his pose, lounging against some crimson cushions laid out on the ground, and laughed up at her. "So very sorry, Madame Artiste! We cannot have the light change, can we?"

Elizabeth frowned at him, but she could not truly be angry. Not on such a very splendid day. The sunlight filtered through the branches of the trees, casting a pale golden glow over the scene before her. The carpet spread on the ground, the array of fruits and cheeses and wines, and the man who laughed up at her were all sparkling in the Italian sunlight.

In the distance, she could see their villa, and Bianca airing the laundry out of an upstairs window. Georgina had set her easel up on the terrace, and she was near enough that Elizabeth could make out the pink of her shawl. But it felt as if she and Nicholas were all alone in some enchanted land out of time, with only a few sheep to watch the progress of her portrait.

The subject of the painting rolled onto his back and beckoned to her with one long, tanned hand. "You have been working far too hard for such a lovely day, Madame Artiste. Should you not take a respite and try one of Bianca's delightful apricot tarts?" He picked up one of the pastries, and bit into it with such relish that some of the apricot ran down his beard-shadowed chin. He had not shaved for two days, since Elizabeth had arrived in the country, and it gave him a delightful, piratical air she was trying to capture on canvas.

"Mmm!" he murmured. "Do try one!"

Elizabeth could not resist leaning down to kiss away the sticky fruit, but she pulled back with a laugh when his arm encircled her waist. "I should take a rest before you eat them all! You have already devoured all of the sandwiches."

"And who ate every bit of sole almondine at supper last night, before the plate even came to my end of the table?"

"Touché." She wiped her hands on a paint-stained rag, and sat down beside him, tilting her head back to let the warmth of the sun flood over her face.

When Nicholas shifted to rest his head on her lap, her fingers crept into his silky curls. She closed her eyes and inhaled deeply of the fragrance of wine, grass, paint, and Nicholas's own evergreen soap.

She had never been so deliciously, madly full of scream-out-loud joy. Not simply ordinary joy, as when she completed a particularly fine painting or held a baby against her heart and smelled its milky scent, but dance-around-naked, full-to-bursting, life-is-perfect joy.

A warm day, a canvas on her easel, and this man's head on her lap was all it took to make life absolute perfection.

"Have you ever been so happy?" she whispered, almost to herself.

His hand swept gently around her waist, warm and secure. "Only once before."

Elizabeth's eyes opened. "Once?"

"With Mariah." His lips curled in a smile that was sweet with remembrance—and with teasing.

"And who is Mariah?"

"Oh, the love of my life. She was an angel of perfection, with golden curls and adorable freckles, right here." He lazily tapped the end of Elizabeth's nose.

Freckles! "Oh? And where is this angel now?"

"I have no idea. We had a hideous falling-out, and she left me flat." Nicholas sighed. "My life has never been the same." He buried his nose deeper in her muslin skirts. "It is too pitiful to recall."

Elizabeth frowned suspiciously. "Just when was this falling-out with the love of your life, precisely?"

"I was seven, she was nine. An older woman. I put a mouse down the back of her dress and she never spoke to me again."

"You beast!" Elizabeth laughed, beating him across the shoulders with a folded napkin. "Here I was all prepared to feel sorry for you, and you were telling such a Banbury tale!"

"Every word is true, I assure you. My life has been desolate of romance since Mariah."

"Now, why do I doubt that? Was there ever truly a Mariah?"

"Certainly there was. She was our cook's daughter. I was quite mad for her."

A silence fell. "You had a cook when you were growing up? Servants?"

"Yes, of course. There was the butler..." Nicholas sat up, and looked at her warily. "Yes. We had servants. My pockets were not always to let."

"Are your pockets to let now?"

"Of course. I am working as your secretary, am I not?"

"Of course." Elizabeth framed his face in her

hands, forcing him to look at her steadily, not laugh and turn away. "Nicholas, tell me about your family."

He did try to turn away, but she had him well and truly caught. "It is not very diverting," he answered.

"I do not care about being diverted. I simply want to know about your family, your home."

Nicholas moved away from her. "I am a bastard," he abruptly announced.

Elizabeth's eyes widened in shock. "A bastard?" She shook her head. "I take it you are not speaking metaphorically."

"Quite literally, I'm afraid. My father neglected to marry my mother."

"I see."

He rushed on in the face of her silence, before he could lose all his nerve. "My father was already betrothed, you see, when my mother came up enceinte, and he refused to break off his engagement. His fiancée was the daughter of a marquis, and my mother's father was only a well-to-do cit. But my father did his duty to us, oh yes. When my mother's family cast her out, he set us up in our house in London. I had tutors, a pony, and later school and even Oxford, a commission in the Army. He even acknowledged me, gave me a place in Society. He did his duty—more than his duty, some would say."

Nicholas spoke evenly, perfunctorily, but his features were tight with the strain of recalling his youth. Elizabeth wiped at her eyes with the napkin. "I would say not! Your father had a duty to love you! To be your father. And in that he failed miserably."

Nicholas shook his head. "He had another family to be father to, a wife and three respectable daughters, who all married well and set up their nurseries, just as they ought. I was an embarrassment, a mistake who refused to fade quietly into the background. I was wild, I flaunted myself all around Town with my racing curricle and my mistresses. I decided if he was going to hate me, it would be for a damned good reason."

"No!" Elizabeth was crying in earnest now, her heart breaking for the lonely boy he had been, the lonely man she was only now being allowed to glimpse. She knew all too well the heartbreak families could cause one another, when they were meant to be the ones who loved each other the most. So upset was she that she did not even blush at the mention of his mistresses. "He could not have hated you, Nicholas. No one who knows you could hate you."

"You should hate me, Elizabeth."

"Why? Because you were not born in wedlock? Believe me, my family is hardly of pristine reputation." She threw herself upon him, clinging when he would have moved away. She forced him to look at her. "And you should know me better than that, Nicholas! I never judge people by their appearances, their families, or their fortunes. I have seen that in my own life, and it caused me nothing but pain. I can only judge by what is in a person's heart. You have a beautiful heart. You have made the sun shine in my life every day since I met you."

"Elizabeth, no."

She pressed her fingertips to his mouth, stopping his protests. "No. Your father was wrong, very wrong to treat you as he did, and one day he will know that. But I would never play you false, Nicholas. I would never push you to the background. I know too well what that is about. You and I, we are meant to live in the forefront of life, always."

"Elizabeth! Beautiful Lizzie." He crushed her

against him, his face buried against her neck, his tears wet on her skin. "You should know how much I deserve your scorn, but I could never bear it if you looked at me with hatred, God forgive me."

"I could never look upon you with hatred. I love you."

He looked up at her shining face, her eyes glowing silver. "Say it again!" he begged.

"I love you." She turned his face up to hers and kissed him on his cheek. "I love you, Nicholas, come what may. We are two of a kind, I knew it when I saw you at that masked ball. I have been waiting for you forever."

"I love you, too, my Lizzie. Always remember that, always. My heart is yours no matter what may happen."

Elizabeth turned to the sun, and laughed and laughed. "And my heart is yours, whatever comes. But what can come between us now? We love each other, do we not? Nothing can change that."

"I pray you are right."

"I am right. Unless you have a mad wife in the garret, as in one of Georgina's horrid novels?"

Nicholas laughed reluctantly. "No wives of any sort."

"Then we shall be together always. Nothing can part us now that you have given me your heart, and I have given you mine."

"Nothing." And Nicholas clutched her close against him.

13

"WILL YOU GO OUT TONIGHT, my lord?"

Peter did not even turn from his window, where he was watching people gather around one of Rome's famed fountains as night drew near. "Out? Where would I go out to?"

"I merely saw the letters on the table, my lord, and thought perhaps..."

"Ah, yes. Lord Braithwaite is in residence here, and invited me to a small dinner he is having tonight. I had not thought to attend, but perhaps you are right, Simmons. I should renew his lordship's acquaintance."

"Very good, my lord. Shall I lay out the blue coat?"

Peter nodded briefly, and turned away again.

He had decided to make the short stop in Rome on his route to Venice. Carnivale was over in the Serene City, and most of the English in residence there had fled the somberness after the recent bacchanalia. There were many English in Rome, and he had had hopes that someone would know Elizabeth, tell him where she had gone.

Thus far he had found no one who recognized Elizabeth's miniatures, and no one he could claim an acquaintance with, except the corpulent old Lord Braithwaite.

Thus this evening's festivities, though he was not feeling in the least sociable. Someone had to have seen her at some time. She could not simply have vanished, though it appeared to be so. Elizabeth was just gone. She could be in India or China, for all he knew. Along with Old Nick Hollingsworth.

"Damn him," Peter whispered. "If he thinks he can thwart me, he is much mistaken."

"I COULD SCARCE BELIEVE it when dear old Braithwaite told me you were in Italy! Imagine, an earl, right here in the midst of our little society."

Peter grimaced, and nodded vaguely to his dinner partner. Lady Deake, yellow curls bobbing and jeweled fingers flashing, had not paused for breath during the soup or fish courses. She showed absolutely no signs of slowing now that the roast lamb was on their plates. Not even Peter's distant replies and glazed eyes could stop her.

It was his most dreaded nightmare, being trapped at a dinner party with indifferent food, watered wines, an overheated room, and a dull dinner partner. It was almost worse than Spain.

"Of course, we have met before," Lady Deake continued, pausing only for a refreshing sip of wine. "At the Borthwick ball last Season. You were there with that dashing Lady Ashby!"

"Oh?"

"Yes. That was before my dear Arthur's passing. It was quite the crush, but I distinctly remember your arrival. Lady Ashby was wearing..." One long, buffed nail tapped at her chin. "Red velvet! Yes. And those famous rubies of hers." She tapped playfully at Peter's wrist with one of those nails. "Which you were rumored to have given her!"

"Oh?" Peter vaguely remembered the ball, one of many he had plunged into after Elizabeth's departure, in the hopes that activity would distract his mind. He remembered Angela Ashby, and her cloying French perfume. But fortunately, he had no recollection of this woman.

"And here you are tonight! Such a coincidence." Evelyn popped a sugared almond into her mouth and tried to smile at him alluringly as she chewed. "And I hear you are for Venice after this! I live there. What takes you to my corner of Italy?"

Peter doubted she could claim quite all of Venice as "hers," but he merely smiled tightly. He saw their host's prized Leonardo painting of the Madonna over Lady Deake's head. The Holy Mother's dark hair, parted sleekly in the center and brushed behind her ears, reminded him of Elizabeth. "I am here for art, Lady Deake."

"Indeed! Well, this is certainly the place for paintings and such. You must visit my home when you are in Venice. There are some fine frescoes in the main drawing room."

"Yes?"

"Yes. They are by, oh, I can never recall his name. V something."

Peter had never in his cynical life so longed to snicker impolitely at someone. He touched the damask napkin to his lips. "Verrocchio?"

"Oh, no, that is not it. I am quite sure."

"Vignola?"

"No."

"Veronese." Peter was swiftly running out of V names.

Evelyn brightened. "Yes! That is the one. I have just engaged an artist to undertake the restoring of them; they are in quite shocking condition. They are old, you know."

"I guessed."

Evelyn tittered. "It is a female artist I have engaged!"

Peter froze. His fork, laden with lamb, was suspended in midair. For the first time that evening, he gave his full attention to his dinner partner. "Female artist?"

"It is very scandalous, I know. But she and her sister are all the crack now. Simply everyone wants them to paint their portraits."

"How very fascinating, Lady Deake." Peter gave her one of his rare, prized smiles. "Or may I call you Evelyn?"

Evelyn gaped at him. "Well, yes. If you like, Peter."

"Now, Evelyn, do tell me more about these sister artists."

"Well. The one I have engaged is the younger. She is quite small and plain, with hair as dark as these Italians. She is not at all like the elder, who is as tall as an Amazon, with wild red hair. I hear she is quite well known in England, though. And they have this secretary, who everyone knows must be more than simply the secretary..."

14

BIANCA HAD QUITE OUTDONE herself, preparing a divine risotto with prosciutto, and a fine lemon trifle for dessert. Georgina and Elizabeth had worn two of their prettiest dinner gowns. There was a good wine from the neighboring vineyard, and it flowed amid much conversation and laughter.

When the trifle had been eaten, the ladies did not retire and leave Nicholas to his port. Instead, they joined him, and sipped at the ruby-red wine while enjoying the soft breeze from the open doors.

"Ah, Georgie." Elizabeth sighed. "Is this not better than going to Rome, as you originally wished?"

"It is." Georgina swirled the port in her glass, its depths the same color as her velvet gown. "Rome would be much too crowded at this time of year, and we would have had far too many social obligations. I like this quiet family life."

Elizabeth, too, liked the idea of that family. She had not felt a part of such a thing since her mother and stepfather died, perhaps not even before that tragic accident. She had felt herself apart, alone. Now she felt alone no longer. All the shattered, scattered pieces of her life had now seemingly come together to form a new, wonderful whole.

She laid one of her hands over Nicholas's, and smiled. "Yes, this is very nice indeed. I can't recall a finer supper, ever."

"But perhaps Nicholas finds us rather dull," Georgina said, laughter in her voice. "Perhaps he is quite missing the gay life of the city?"

"Not at all, I assure you." Nicholas lifted Elizabeth's hand for a brief kiss. "The energy of you two lovely ladies has exhausted me utterly. I am glad of the country respite."

"But do you not miss all your admirers, Georgie?" said Elizabeth. "All the posies and billets-doux? As the post comes only once a week here, we shall hear nothing from Signor Franco or Mr. Butler or any of the others for several days at least."

"Excellent! If I never hear from either of them again it will be far too soon."

"But I thought you quite liked the signor!" Elizabeth exclaimed.

"I did rather, when I thought him merely an amusing dinner partner. That all ended when he proposed to me at the Vincenzis' party."

"Oh, no!" Elizabeth groaned.

Nicholas was a bit puzzled. He was accustomed to young English ladies, such as his half-sisters, who schemed and plotted and would stop at almost nothing to procure proposals from gentlemen.

But then, when had Georgina and Elizabeth ever behaved as his half-sisters did?

"This is a bad thing?" he said.

"Terrible!" answered Elizabeth. "It means that Signor Franco will never see the inside of our drawing room again."

Nicholas looked at Georgina. "Do you never wish to wed again, Georgina?"

Georgina shook her head. "Have you ever been married, Nicholas?"

Elizabeth glanced at him sharply. "No," he replied. "I do not believe so."

"Then never do so," Georgina said firmly. "Unless it is to Lizzie. Marriage to her would be quite out of the common way."

"Georgie, please!" Elizabeth laughed.

"It is true," Georgina protested. "And I suppose everyone should be married once, if only to see what it is like. But as for me, I shall not marry again."

"Georgie is quite determined to end her days the merry widow," said Elizabeth, tipping the last of the port into her glass.

"Yes," said Georgina. "I shall spend my dotage in oh, Bath, I think, painting awful seascapes and shouting rude things at handsome young men in the Pump Room."

"And may we join you in your dignified retirement?" Nicholas asked, with a great grin.

"Oh, yes, certainly. Lizzie and I shall push you about in your bath chair, and play matchmaker to your ten children."

"Georgina Beaumont!" Elizabeth protested with a blush.

"I am merely teasing, Lizzie. I am certain you will have only three. And by the time we are doddering about Bath, it will be time for your grandchildren's come-outs." Georgina drained the last of her port, and rose to her feet. "Now, I must retire or I shall fall asleep in what is left of this excellent trifle. Good night, my dears."

"Good night, Georgie," Elizabeth called.

Nicholas resumed his seat, and took Elizabeth's hand between both of his. "Your sister is an extraordinary woman."

"She is. And, despite her protestations, I do believe she will wed again."

"Do you?"

"Yes. She is far too romantic not to. It will take a very special man indeed, though."

"Oh? And do you have a candidate in mind for her?"

"Hmm. But not you, Nicholas. You are already spoken for."

"I am that." He leaned closer to her, so close that she could feel his warmth through her gown and shawl, against her skin. Her eyes began to drift shut.

But to her great disappointment, he did not kiss her.

"Will you walk with me in the garden, Elizabeth?" he asked instead.

"I thought you would never ask."

Arm in arm, they strolled out of the dining room and down the terrace steps to the garden. It was almost a full moon, and the trees and the barely awakening flowers were bathed in silver. Their footsteps crushed blossoms into the walkways, releasing their sweet scent into the air.

A small, cool breeze had crept up, and Elizabeth in her thin silk dinner gown leaned closer to Nicholas for warmth.

"It is almost like the night we met," she mused. "The moonlight, the scent of the flowers."

"But there is no canal," he said. "No masked ball, no gondolas."

"This is much more pleasant. It is only us."

"Elizabeth." He stopped and caught her arm, turning her about to face him. "I brought you out here to talk to you. I must tell you something."

She stared up at him. His face was drawn and serious, not a hint of sparkle in his dark eyes. "What is wrong, Nicholas? Are you ill?"

"No. I simply must—must speak with you, before we can go on. There is something I have to tell you."

Her eyes dropped. This was a moment she had been dreading. A moment of revelation. Of judgment.

"I must tell you something, as well," she said.

"You, Elizabeth?"

"Yes." She turned from him, and went to sit on a marble bench beside a statue of a cavorting Cupid. She stared up at the moon, and thought of Peter and of the dead duke. She hardly knew where to begin. And she did not truly want to begin at all. She wanted their lives to go on as they had been ever since they had met, full of laughter.

She had suffered so much, and only tonight had she come to feel truly secure, truly in the midst of a real family at last. Did she not deserve this time of joy, however fragile, however brief?

"Yes, I do," she whispered. *And I cannot allow anything to harm this time, to spoil it.*

"What did you say, Elizabeth?" Nicholas sat beside her on the bench.

"I merely said that I do have things to tell you. Many things. But not tonight, please. Tonight is too beautiful."

"But, Elizabeth..."

"No." She pressed her finger to his lips. "Tomorrow is time enough for reality. Or the day after. Tonight I only want you to hold me. Please, Nicholas, just hold me against you, as if you would never let me go."

Nicholas gathered her against him, his cheek pressed to the softness of her hair. He inhaled her sweet, precious scent, and all seemed peaceful and perfect in their small comer of Eden.

But his mind was shouting one word. *Coward.* But she only wanted to be happy a little longer.

"SOMEONE SEEMS VERY HAPPY THIS MORNING!" Georgina said, around a mouthful of hairpins. She smiled at her friend as Elizabeth leaned against her open window, humming and plaiting her hair.

"Someone?" Elizabeth said. "You could not mean me!"

"Oh, no. You are just the little lark singing love songs all morning long."

"It must be all the fresh country air."

"And a fine gentleman. What did happen in the garden last night?" Georgina pushed the last of the pins into her coiffure of deliberately disarranged curls, and stood to button up her morning dress. "I know when romance is afoot in my very house."

Elizabeth laughed aloud. "Oh, Georgie! He loves me. He told me yesterday on our picnic, and I have been aching to tell you ever since."

"Oh!" Georgina shrieked, running to clasp Elizabeth in an exuberant embrace. "I knew it! I absolutely knew it. I could tell from your faces at dinner last night. Tell me, how did you answer him?"

"Well..." Elizabeth sat down on the edge of Georgina's unmade bed and kicked her bare feet idly. "Actually, I declared myself first."

"You didn't!"

"I did, and I have no regrets, not a whit. He had just confided in me, you see. About his past. You were right that there was more to him than seemed, Georgie. He had such a miserable childhood. I was crying, and he had his head on my lap, and I just could not seem to help myself. The words just poured out."

"And?"

"And then he said that he loved me, too, and that nothing could ever be allowed to come between us. And it will not."

"What of your fears before? About your brother, and your true identity?" Georgina sat down beside her, her forehead creased in concern.

Elizabeth waved an airy hand. "That is all forgotten."

"Then you told Nicholas of what happened?"

"Well, no. Not precisely." Elizabeth looked away. "I tried to, last night in the garden, but it was so wonderful. I didn't want to spoil it."

"Then you will tell him?"

"Oh, yes. Of course. When the right time presents itself. But I am far too happy here to bring that ugliness to this lovely place. What harm can it do to wait just a bit longer? Until we are back in Venice?"

Georgina looked doubtful, but all she said was, "Whatever you think best, Lizzie."

"Yes. And I will have to tell him soon. My real name will be on the marriage lines, will it not?"

"Marriage?" Georgina gasped. "Has he proposed?"

"Not yet! Not yet. But I think he very soon will."

They shrieked in unison, and threw their arms about each other in a flurry of ribbons and lace.

"The yellow silk we saw in Signora Benini's shop window last month!" Georgina cried, ever the planner. "It would be utter perfection, Lizzie, with yellow roses in your hair."

Elizabeth giggled, and swept the sheet off the bed. She twirled it over her head like a bridal veil and marched about the room humming a stately pavane. "It would be wonderful! Oh, but we mustn't plan yet, Georgie. It would be ill luck."

"Hey-ho!" Nicholas's shout floated up through the open window. "Is someone being murdered up there, with all that shouting?"

Elizabeth ran to the window, the sheet still clasped about her head, and waved down at him. He was handsome and smiling in the morning sunshine, his strong throat revealed in the open-throated peasant shirt he wore, with a simple knotted red kerchief. He was her gypsy prince. "Not at all!" she answered. "I was merely deciding on what to wear today."

"I think what you are wearing now is charming."

Elizabeth looked down, and saw she still wore her night rail under the trailing sheet. She stepped back. "Rogue! Wait right there. I shall be down directly."

"Do not be very long. The light is just right for viewing the ruins."

"I said I would be there directly! Be patient."

"'Tis twenty years till then!"

"You have been reading Shakespeare again!" She blew him a kiss from her fingertips, and withdrew from the window, closing it against his protestations. "Such a rake." She sighed and reached for the blue dress of Georgina's she was borrowing for the day.

Pausing only to button it up and reach for her slippers, she waved at Georgina and danced out the door to where Nicholas was waiting with their picnic hamper.

"There she is at last, my Juliet." He lifted her by her waist, twirling her about and about until the sky tilted drunkenly and her skirts flew about her knees.

"You shall have to set me on my feet, Romeo, before I cast up my accounts all over your fine shirt!" She laughed, clutching at his shoulders in her dizziness.

"And we can't have that, now can we?" Nicholas lowered her to the ground, his hands warm and safe on her waist. For a moment, he clasped her to him, so close and tight it was almost painful.

"Nicholas?" Elizabeth stepped back a bit, frightened that whatever had been about to be said last night was going to haunt their day again. "Is something amiss?"

He only smiled faintly, and wrapped a long strand of her black hair around his finger. He studied it closely, as if he had never seen such hair before. "Amiss? What could possibly be amiss, on such a day as this? I have apricot tarts in my hamper, and a lovely girl on my arm, and the Italian sky above me." He laughed, and danced her around in a circle. "You see, dear, I have even begun to wax poetical today."

Elizabeth laughed obligingly. "Byron need have no fears of his new rival, I think." She linked her arm in his, and led him toward the pathway that went to the old Roman ruins. "It is a fine day, just as every day has been since we came here. I vow I have never stopped smiling, even in my sleep! I even have sweet dreams here."

"Then we shall have to come here very often indeed."

"Yes, we shall." Elizabeth paused to examine an

oleander bush. "But sometimes, Nicholas, I think I... that is..."

"Yes, dear? You think what?"

It had to be said. "Sometimes I feel as if you did not completely share in this happiness."

Nicholas was silent a very long moment. He held Elizabeth's hand but he did not look at her. "Wise Elizabeth," he said at last. "There is something. But you were correct last night in saying that this is not the place for such things. It is far too lovely. You are too lovely to have your holiday marred in any way. And what I have to say is not so urgent."

"But you will tell me?" she whispered. *Just as I must tell you.*

Instead of answering, he raised her fingers to his lips. "We are being far too serious for such a day! This is a day meant for frivolity of the most blatant sort. Were we not going to view the ruins?"

Elizabeth looked around at the warm sun, the sapphire sky, the flowers just beginning to peek from the ground. It was a lovely day. Misgivings still lurked in her mind, but she shrugged them away and smiled. "I have a much better idea."

"Oh? And what is that idea?"

"A swim."

"Now?"

"This instant!" Elizabeth hurried off down the twisting pathway that led to the sparkling sea, tugging Nicholas by the hand behind her. "Or are you frightened?"

That was a challenge Nicholas had never been able to let pass by. "Scared? I was a champion rower at school, I will have you know. And I took more than one spill into the Thames, which was considerably colder than this little pond."

"Good. Then perhaps you can keep up with me!"

They reached the shore, where gentle pale-blue waves, tipped with white, lapped at the rocky sand. Elizabeth shed her shoes and stockings, and reached for the buttons of her gown.

Nicholas laughed at her utter audacity. "Are you going in the altogether?"

"Certainly not! I am a lady." Her gown joined the pile of clothing, along with her single petticoat. "I will wear my chemise."

Nicholas was utterly unable to look away as she turned and waded into the water, disappearing little by little until only her seal-dark head was visible above the waves.

Nicholas had seen her bare legs that night on the terrace in Venice, and her decolletage was revealed in many a ball gown, but that had always been at night, dark. In moonlight, Elizabeth was lovely.

In sunlight, she was incomparable.

Her legs were not long, but they were slender and white, her feet elegantly arched as they kicked behind her. He wished he had her skill with a paintbrush—then he could capture her forever, just as she was this moment. A mermaid frolicking in the Mediterranean surf.

"Are you not coming in, champion rower?" she called. "The water is cool, but wonderful!" She beckoned to him, revealing the enticing sheerness of her wet garment.

Nicholas, frozen in place for those long moments, suddenly sprang into motion His clothes joined hers on the sand, and he swam out toward her until he could grasp her waist. He lifted her high against him, kissing the seawater saltiness of her lips until she gasped.

"I love you," he whispered, staring up into her shining eyes, the sunlit corona of her hair. "I love you, and I wish that this day, this moment, would never end."

"It won't." She pulled his head back to hers, kissing him in return. "We will not let it end. Ever."

15

VENICE

"SIGNORINA, YOU MUST WAKE up!"

Elizabeth burrowed deeper beneath the bedclothes, trying to escape from Bianca's ever-more insistent voice. Since their return to Venice three days ago, when Nicholas had carried her, giggling, over the threshold, she had not retired once before dawn. She had been sitting on the terrace the night before, drinking champagne and gossiping with Nicholas and Georgina until the sun had been quite high. It felt as though she had only just fallen asleep, and she was loath to have her delicious dream interrupted.

"Oh, do go away, Bianca!" She groaned. "It is hardly morning."

"But, signorina, there is a visitor! Such a visitor." Bianca rolled her eyes.

"A visitor? So early?" Elizabeth groaned again. It was very likely some patron who was not happy with their portrait, or one of Georgina's spurned suitors. All their artist friends would be still abed, as all sensible people should be. "Go and wake Georgina. Or Nicholas."

"Signora Georgina is already downstairs, and Signor Nicholas is not at home."

Georgina, awake and downstairs before noon? And Nicholas out already, after their late night? Very odd. "Where is Nicholas, Bianca?"

"I do not know. He said he had an errand, and would be back for breakfast."

Elizabeth opened one eye to peer up at the maid. "And who is this caller?"

Bianca shrugged. "I do not know. He would not give his name, but he is *molto* handsome."

"He?"

"Yes, and he is asking for you, but Signora Georgina, she says you are not to be disturbed and he must go away."

Curiouser and curiouser. Elizabeth swung her legs out of bed and reached for her dressing gown. "What does this man look like? Aside from being *molto* handsome."

"Oh, tall, as tall as Signor Nicholas. And golden. And very elegant."

Tall, golden, and elegant. Could it be...? Elizabeth turned quite as white as her sheets. "I must be found out," she whispered.

"Signorina?"

Elizabeth shook her head. "Hand me my slippers, Bianca. I must greet our guest."

As if in a daze, she brushed her hair and tied it back with a piece of ribbon, donned her slippers, and made her way down the stairs with Bianca fluttering behind her.

It was as she had feared, as she had dreamed on many a disturbed night. Georgina stood before the empty grate, still wearing her night rail, and brandishing a fireplace poker at the Earl of Clifton.

Peter was elegant, every bit as elegant as she remembered. He quite overpowered their rented room in his doeskin breeches and many-caped greatcoat. He stood behind her writing desk, his hat and walking stick resting atop some of her sketches of Katerina Bruni. His gloves slapped rhythmically against his thigh.

He quite looked as if he owned the place, and they were merely his recalcitrant servants. Two years might almost never have passed.

Except that she was different now. She no longer would stammer and blush and cry before his coldness. She was free. She was a woman who had made her own way in the world, and was no longer a little girl.

Was she not?

"Good morning, Peter," she said coolly, as if it had not been so very long since they had seen each other —as if they might have dined just the night before. She took the poker from Georgina's hand, placed it back beside the grate, and drew her glowering friend firmly to her side. "And what brings you to Venice at such a quiet time of year?"

"Why, the charming weather, of course." He gestured with his gloves to the steady, silver rain outside the windows. "Such a vast improvement on English rain."

"I am certain you will notice no difference when you have returned to England." *Where you belong*, she added silently. "When will you be returning?"

"I shall be back beside my own cozy hearth very soon. When you have packed your trunks, dear sister, we shall be gone from here."

Georgina surged forward. "Why, you bas—"

Elizabeth grasped Georgina's hand tighter, holding her back from scoring Peter's golden features with her wicked nails. "I am afraid that is impossible, brother dear. My home is here now, and I cannot abandon my work."

"Oh, I think not."

A knot of ice slowly formed in Elizabeth's belly as she watched Peter remove a sealed document from inside his coat. She watched in a haze as he laid the paper on the desk.

"I am still your guardian, Elizabeth. Until you reach your twenty-first birthday, which, if I am not mistaken, is almost a year away. Those were the terms of our parents' will."

"This is absurd!" Elizabeth whispered.

"Oh, my dear, it could not be less absurd. I have here a magistrate's order, giving you into my care." He glanced about their dim, dusty drawing room, littered with canvases and sketches. "And you obviously need my care, Elizabeth. No gently reared woman in her right mind would choose to live such a disordered life. If you do not come home with me now, your friends could be brought up on charges of kidnapping."

"What?" Elizabeth cried, utterly shocked. All the times she had tried to imagine what would happen if Peter found her, she had never envisioned this, threatening her friends.

"No, Lizzie!" Georgina seized Elizabeth's arm, and drew her into the empty corridor, whispering furiously, "You must not go with him. Who knows what will happen? Something quite dreadful, to be sure. He cannot be in his right mind to come here like this, barking unreasonable orders, taking over your life."

"Georgie, I must. I have no choice. I would never see you in such trouble for my sake. The scandal could mean the end of your career. If I go away quietly, you can put it about that I am ill and have gone away to-to Switzerland or someplace, to recover."

"Never! I do not care about all that. What are some old portraits I'm finishing to your safety? You are my own sister, Lizzie; I would die if any harm befell you. And you are not safe with that man!" Georgina shook her head fiercely. "I never liked him, even when all the girls at Miss Thompson's were swooning over him. He was too cool by half."

Elizabeth turned away and leaned her forehead against the wall, closing her eyes tightly. What to do, what to do? Of course she could not stay and see anyone arrested and put in the clink on her behalf. Yet how could she simply pack her things and leave meekly with Peter? How could she leave her work, go back to Clifton Manor, where so many memories waited?

How could she go back to that staid English country life, after Italy?

She shuddered just to think of the old vicar, the Misses Allan, Lord and Lady Haversham with their deadly dull "salons."

And, worst of all, how could she ever leave Nicholas?

Nicholas.

Elizabeth slowly opened her eyes and stared sightlessly at the white plaster of the wall as the worst, the most hideous thought fluttered through her mind like an insidious whisper.

No. Nicholas could have nothing to do with all of this. Simply because he had disappeared from the house the very morning Peter appeared.

But Nicholas loved her! Did he not? Those weeks in the country had been the most glorious of her life, and his adoring attentions had told her he felt the same. Surely his kisses, his sweet words, did not lie? And then, how could he even know Peter? An artist's secretary, a bastard son, would never have occasion to meet the Earl of Clifton, let alone conspire with him in such a way. Surely it could not be.

But how well did she truly know Nicholas, a tiny voice whispered in the back of her mind. She knew the feel of his arms, his kisses, how he moved with her so perfectly when they danced. He had told her of his father, but she did not know who that father was, how Nicholas had come to be in Italy, how he dressed so fashionably if he had to seek employment. She sank onto the nearest chair, her knees suddenly too weak to support her, her head in her hands as these unwelcome thoughts chased around her mind. If she loved Nicholas, how could she even suspect him? She had given him her heart and her very soul; she could not be such a poor judge of character. No artist could be.

It all had to be a ridiculous coincidence.

But then how did Peter know where to find her?

She had been so very careful all these years. Apparently not nearly careful enough.

"It cannot be," she whispered. "He loves me."

"What did you say, Lizzie?" Georgina leaned over her. "Are you quite well? Shall I have Bianca fetch some brandy?"

"No, no brandy. I must keep my head about me. I shall be well presently."

"Are you certain?"

"Yes. Georgie, have you seen Nicholas at all this morning?"

Georgina frowned in thought. "No, not at all."

"Bianca told me he went out quite early."

"Blast! If only he were here " Georgina's voice trailed away. "No. Oh, Lizzie, no, of course it was not Nicholas who betrayed your whereabouts. He—"

"He what? He loves me?"

"He does love you! I know the way he looks at you, Lizzie. He would never conspire with Peter Everdean against you this way."

Elizabeth shook her head. "I do hope you are right. But I cannot be sure of anything now, the world is so havey cavey all of a sudden."

"You can be sure of me. I will not let him take you away, not when your career is so promising before you."

"Georgie, my dearest friend, what choice do we have? He only wants me to go to England with him, for some unfathomable reason. He doesn't really want you arrested. And it is only until I am twenty-one, less than a year away. A year of rusticating could hardly do me any harm. Then I can come back here. Or maybe go to India, or America!"

"America! Oh, Lizzie, we should go there now. He will lock you up. He will force you to marry. He will—"

"Georgie," Elizabeth interrupted firmly. "I escaped him before, I will again. All will be well." She clung to her friend's hand. "All will be well."

Georgina was quiet for a long moment. "You will write every day?"

"Every, every day! And I shall paint every day, even if I have to do a portrait of Lady Haversham's poodles." Elizabeth stood and smoothed back her hair, trying to bring some composure back to her countenance. "Now, I shall tell Peter to return to his hotel, or wherever he came from, and wait for us to send him word that I am ready to depart. That should bring us a little time, at least. Bianca is such a slow packer."

"Yes. And if all else fails, we could always have Nicholas challenge Peter to a duel!"

Elizabeth could not help but laugh at the vision of Peter and Nicholas, in their fine coats and polished boots, facing off across a Venetian square filled with pigeons.

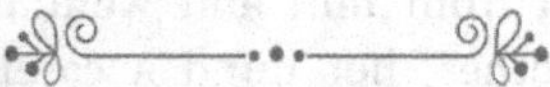

HER COMPOSURE LASTED ONLY until she had dismissed Peter and gone up to her bedroom. As she closed the door behind her, the first sight she saw was Nicholas's half-finished portrait, propped on its easel in the corner.

She went to it, and traced the painted dark curls with her fingertip, moving over his eyes and his smile.

His wonderful, dazzling, mischievous smile. She turned away from the painting. Even if he were a deceiver, she could not stop loving him just like that, in an instant. He had brought true laughter into her life, brought life into her life, when she had thought her whole self given over only to art. That could never fade, no matter what came. Could it?

"Forever, you said," she murmured. "But I have not time for such fancies now. I must think. Think!" She took her small traveling trunk, only just unpacked from the country, and began carefully, slowly folding her undergarments and night rails and tucking them inside. Her day dresses went in, her hats and slippers. All her gowns had been taken from the wardrobe and piled on the bed when the longed-for but dreaded knock came at her door.

And when she opened it to see Nicholas's pale, haunted face, she knew the truth.

His wild gaze went past her to the open trunk, the pile of gowns. "What are you doing, Elizabeth?" he croaked, his voice hoarse and broken, nothing like his usual laughter-filled tones.

She turned from him and went back to slowly folding her clothes, her mind a careful blank. She forced herself to concentrate on the dresses in her hands, the feel of silk and muslin, the scent of the lavender sachets she tucked into the folds. She did not want to think of the man behind her. She did not want to either love him or hate him.

"I am packing, of course," she answered. "Surely you must know I am going on a voyage, Nicholas. If that is your name." She clutched a fur-trimmed pelisse to her bosom dramatically, feeling more and more like some melodramatic Minerva Press heroine.

"It *is* my name, blast it!" Then his stillness shattered. He grabbed her shoulders, forcing her to face him, to look up into his eyes. "I did not lie about that."

Elizabeth wanted to sob, to collapse on the floor and howl with the agony of it. She wanted to beat him with her fists, to kick him until he felt as much pain as she did. Until that instant she had clung to hope, but now it was irretrievably gone. "You did come here because of Peter."

Nicholas's hands tightened on her arms, as if he feared she would disappear in a puff of smoke if he let her go. He nodded slowly.

"Did he pay you?" she asked softly.

"No! Lizzie, it was not like that!"

She did cry then, at the sound of her nickname on his lips, hot, silent tears that fell unchecked down her chin and spotted her bodice. "Then what was it like, Nicholas? What could possibly have induced you to be so unspeakably cruel? To ruin all my hopes? Tell me! Damn you, tell me why."

Her careful control was quickly slipping away. Nicholas led her to the dressing table and forced her to sit, kneeling before her like the veriest supplicant before his empress. He held her hands between his, and she was too wrapped in misery to snatch them back.

"I knew Peter years ago," Nicholas began. "In Spain."

"Spain."

"Yes. We were in the same regiment, and we became friends."

Had anyone ever really been friends with Peter? Elizabeth sniffed, and wiped at her eyes with her sleeve. "So that is your reason? Friendship?"

Nicholas pressed a handkerchief into her hands. "More than mere friendship, Lizzie. Peter saved my very life."

She snorted inelegantly. "Peter? A hero?"

"Yes, he was. I was terribly wounded. You have seen my leg, when we were swimming." He had the grace to blush at the mention of just how much of him she had seen that day. "I would have bled to death there on the battlefield, if he had not carried me miles to the field hospital, fighting off the French every step of the way."

Elizabeth nodded a bit. "I see."

"Do you?" A reluctant hope lit in Nicholas's eyes. "Do you see, Elizabeth, how very much I owed Peter? I thought he was dead, that my debt would forever go unpaid. Until last winter, when I met him again in London."

She drew her hands from his, and turned to the gilt-framed mirror above the dressing table. The white-faced woman there seemed a veritable stranger. "So you discharged your debt. My life for yours on that battlefield."

"Elizabeth, please!" he cried, trying to take her hands again. "I had no idea."

"No idea of what?" She held her hands away from him, folded them before her to still their trembling.

Nicholas sat back on his heels. "That you are who you are."

"What could that possibly mean? Of course I am who I am."

"I was a different person then, Lizzie. I was selfish, wild. I thought surely you had run away in some spoiled pique, that it was all a misunderstanding. That it would be a simple thing to persuade you that it would be best for you to return to England."

"What occurred to make you think otherwise?"

"You, of course. I saw your life here. Your work, your friends. I saw that you were not some pampered, petulant miss—you were a strong-willed person who would not be easily persuaded."

Elizabeth's fist suddenly came down on the table, rattling bottles of scent and pots of rice powder, as anger finally melted the knot of horrible numbness. "So you concocted this ridiculous scheme to insinuate yourself into my life, to pretend to care about me!"

"That part was not a lie." His voice was low and intense, in counterpoint to her white-hot anger. "I do love you. I think I have loved you since I first saw you at that masked ball. You are so unlike anyone I have ever known."

"You say you love me, yet you planned to hand me over like some piece of merchandise to my brother, knowing how I felt about my life here."

"I do not know! I do not know what I would have

done, had the issue been forced on me. I tried to tell you, but I was a coward, I let you put me off. But I vow this to you, Elizabeth—I did not bring Peter here. I have not even been in contact with him since I left England."

Elizabeth's head ached unbearably. She dosed her eyes against all the pain, but it would not be shut out. "I do not know what to believe. I am far too tired to sort all this out right now."

"What will you do?" he asked quietly.

"Go back to England, of course. To spend the next year at Clifton Manor, until I reach my majority and can rejoin Georgina here."

"Lizzie, you don't have to go."

"Yes. I do. I may even decide I want to. There is something rather soothing in the English countryside, is there not? Perhaps I can really think while I am there."

"But I can't let you just leave me like this!" he said softly.

"Oh, Nicholas." She turned back to him, and laid her fingertips against his beloved face. "You have no choice in the matter, and neither do I."

He grasped her fingers, pressing them to his lips. "I will do whatever you say. I only want what will make you happy, you know that. Will you write to me at least?"

"I do not know if I can. I don't even know your true name."

"Sir Nicholas Hollingsworth." A ghost of his former dashing smile whispered across his mouth. "At your service."

Her eyes widened. "Old Nick Hollingsworth?"

"One and the same, I regret to admit. But how did you know of my unfortunate sobriquet?"

"I used to read all the London scandal sheets when I lived at Clifton Manor. You were a favorite subject." She laughed, a mirthless, hollow sound. "Now I understand about Lady Deake and her odd behavior. She threw a glass of champagne in your face at a ball once, did she not? And then fled the scene in tears?"

He looked down at the carpet, his ears crimson among his black curls. "That was a very long time ago."

"Yes," Elizabeth agreed. "A long time ago. I do regret not being the one to restore her Veronese. Perhaps she will hire Georgina." She looked back to the mirror, to watch his reflection in the glass. "I may write to you, if only to hear about the oh-so-dashing life you led, and will probably lead again."

"Will you, Elizabeth? Will you write?"

"Perhaps." She stood and went back to her packing, her spine very straight. "Now I do think you should leave. Before Peter returns, or Georgina comes after you with the andirons."

Nicholas also stood. "I do love you, Elizabeth. That was never a lie, not for an instant. I will always love you."

She sighed. "I don't know how to believe you."

"No." He turned to leave, but she stopped him with a word. "I only hope I can persuade you one day. I will never stop trying."

"Nicholas?"

"Yes?" He swung around in hope, but she merely held out a rather rumpled letter, folded and sealed. "You are not the only one who has harbored secrets," she said. "And for that I am sorry. Please, read this when you are alone, and you will understand."

Nicholas swallowed hard, searching for the words that would make things right between them, that would prove to her the depths of his feelings.

But in the end, there were no words. He pressed a single kiss on her averted cheek and left her standing there, the door clicking shut softly behind him.

"I love you, too, Nicholas," Elizabeth whispered. "And that is the very damnable thing."

"NICHOLAS! WHERE ARE YOU GOING?"

He was almost out of the door, his valise in hand, when Georgina flew downstairs to grab his arm in an iron grasp. She wore a nightgown and a shawl; her feet were bare and her hair loose. She had obviously been crying, as her cheeks were puffy and as red as her wild curls.

Nicholas had never thought to see Elizabeth's glamorous friend so disheveled and distraught. It was another black mark against his character, another life he had wreaked havoc in.

"I am leaving, Mrs. Beaumont," he answered her.

"Leaving? Now?"

"I think it best. Under the circumstances."

"Whatever are you talking about? You must help Elizabeth! You cannot leave now, we need you."

"You have no need of me."

Her eyes were wide, bewildered. "But you love her, do you not? You are to marry her?"

Nicholas almost laughed aloud with the bitterness of it. "I doubt Elizabeth would care to marry me now, since she thinks I have brought such disaster on your house."

Georgina stared up at him in utter disbelief. "This is *your* doing? You were working for Peter all the while?"

Nicholas was too tired to explain again, too exhausted to justify what had truly been unjustifiable. He drew a small velvet jewel case from his coat and pressed it into Georgina's cold hand. "Please, give this to Elizabeth, Mrs. Beaumont, and accept my deepest apologies."

Even when the heavy front doors were between them, he could hear her screaming curses at him in English, Italian, and French, vowing grotesque vengeances on him and all his descendants, like some Amazon of old.

He could tell that all those horrid novels had not gone to waste.

He believed he now knew how Adam had felt, when he was expelled from Paradise by an angel with a flaming sword.

"WELL, well. If it isn't the secretary."

It was quite the last voice Nicholas had wanted to hear, aside from Georgina Beaumont's, when he had come to Florian's with the express wish to become drunk as a bishop. He knocked back his brandy, and closed his eyes against the warm sting. "Get away from me, Peter."

"Or what? You will challenge me to a duel, perhaps?" Peter slid into the chair next to his and signaled to the waiter for another brandy. "I would hardly recommend it. You are quite foxed already, and obviously suicidal. It would be no challenge for me at all, and no way to get back into Elizabeth's good graces. She is quite fond of you, I see, though I scarce could say why."

Nicholas did not answer, or even look at his friend. He stared fixedly out the window at an arguing couple who had paused beneath the portico. The dark-haired woman threw back her head; her hands gesticulated wildly in the air. If there had been a heavy object to hand, she would no doubt have thrown it at her hapless partner's head. The man listened to her in stony silence.

If only Elizabeth had flown at him like that! If she had only railed at him, cursed him, thrown paint pots at his head. Instead she had confronted him in chill calm, icy dignity, her lovely silver eyes grave and dark as slate, unforgiving. He knew from his own experience that such anger, pushed deep down inside, was the very worst sort. It would only fester there, getting colder and larger until her hatred for him overcame all her love.

"You knew," he said, still watching the couple. "You knew that I would fall in love with her."

Peter shrugged. "Certainly I did not know. Contrary to popular belief, I am no sorcerer possessed of the dark arts. Even I cannot know what a person's foolish heart will do."

"Yet you suspected."

"Um, perhaps, yes. I know Elizabeth, and I know

you. Or at least I did once. I knew that your spirits were the same. Wild, and perhaps a bit misguided, but well meaning."

Nicholas's fist clenched around the snifter of brandy. "So this was some sort of test you devised."

"Not at all. Really, Nicholas, you always did make things out to be far more complex than they are. Because you would understand what she was about, I thought you were the one who could persuade her to see reason and give up this silly gypsy life."

"I hardly think her life is silly," Nicholas snapped. "She is a fine artist, a great one even, and she has many clients and a brilliant future."

"You see, my friend? You do understand her."

Nicholas took a deep, steadying breath. "What will you do now? Drag her back to England?"

"I hardly think 'drag' is the right word. That conjures up such images of cavemen. And yes. She will come back to England with me. Was that not the point of this absurd exercise?" Peter sighed, and seemed almost pensive as he looked down into his own glass. "I can try to make her understand, perhaps even forgive me for my behavior, only if we are at home where it is quiet. Here, she is too caught up in her wild ways."

Nicholas's fierce anger, his desire to plant Peter a sound facer, had subsided to a dull roar behind his eyes. All he really had now was an ineffable sadness. He had lost so much in one morning. He had lost everything—his love, his honor, his future. "How am I to make her forgive me?"

Peter gave a strange half smile. "That, Nick, I cannot tell you. Will you also be returning to England?"

"Yes. I could not stay in Venice."

"No. That would not be wise. I hear that Elizabeth's Amazon friend can shoot the ace from a card at fifty paces. I should not like to encounter her in some dark alleyway." Peter drained his brandy and stood. "I want you to know, Nick, that I bear you no ill will for how all this turned out. You will always be welcome at Clifton Manor, should you ever choose to call."

With that, he departed, fading into the milling crowd and leaving Nicholas alone with his drink and his thoughts.

"You may bear me no ill will, Peter," he muttered. "But what of your sister? And what of myself?"

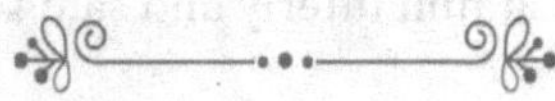

As Elizabeth prepared to step into the boat that would carry her from her one true home, Georgina caught her in one last farewell embrace.

"Georgie," Elizabeth said in a strangled voice. "Write to me very often, and tell me all your doings, every detail. All your commissions, and parties. And tell Stephen I said good-bye."

Georgina wrinkled her nose. "I will tell him, if that is what you want. And you must write to me of all *your* doings."

Elizabeth laughed. "Oh, yes, I shall tell you of the sheep and the grass growing!"

"No, tell me of your painting. I will send all of your work on, and you must not neglect it."

"I will not neglect it. I couldn't."

"Elizabeth," Peter called impatiently. "It grows late."

Elizabeth kissed her friend's cheek one last time. "I will see you soon, Georgie."

"Yes. Perhaps sooner than you think!"

"Do not do anything foolish, such as follow me to Derbyshire! You would hate it there."

"Do something foolish? Me? Never!" Georgina pressed a small box into Elizabeth's gloved hand. "Here."

"What is this? A gift?"

"Yes, but not from me, I fear."

"Then who?"

Georgina's lips tightened. "It is from Nicholas. He asked me to give it to you before he left, right before I lost my temper at him utterly and said some very rude things."

Puzzled, Elizabeth opened the box, and stared down in astonishment.

There, flashing in the late afternoon sunlight, was a sapphire-and-diamond ring A betrothal ring.

For one instant, Elizabeth wanted only to cry out all her grief and disappointment. Then she wanted to fling the thing into the canal.

In the end, she just closed the box and stuffed it into her reticule. Perhaps, one day, when some of the pain had faded, she would want to take it out and remember how, for a brief while, a man had made the sun shine in her life every day.

16

A NEW VOLUME OF POETRY lay open on the lap of Elizabeth's new bishop's-blue carriage dress, and her eyes were cast down upon it, but she had not really read a word in ten miles or more. Nor did she see the green glories of the English countryside that flew past the carriage windows, palest blue sky and hedgerows glistening in the morning mist. She did not see or feel anything at all. She hadn't since the last of Venice's golden spires had faded from her view, and she had sensed herself leaving Elizabeth Cheswood behind and becoming Lady Elizabeth Everdean again.

The voyage had been uneventful, a series of ships and carriages and inns, meals she didn't want to eat, too much wine drunk, and no conversation.

"We should arrive very soon," Peter commented. He looked stylishly bored, as he had for their entire journey, never dusty or rumpled or insulted by her silences. But now his hands twisted and untwisted on the golden head of his fashionable walking stick. "Yes. I can recognize some of the countryside."

Elizabeth cut another page of her book.

"I hope you will be quite comfortable there, at Clifton Manor. Your rooms are just as you left them."

"Yes." Her gloved fingertip traced the printed lines that she did not see.

"And your maid is still employed there. The silly chit refused to leave, even when Lady Haversham tried to hire her away."

"Good. I did miss Daisy." And nothing else there.

Peter smiled coolly, almost as if he sensed the unspoken words that hung between them. "No one to dress your hair properly in Italy?"

"I am quite capable of dressing my own hair, thank you. Daisy was always so very cheerful, though. A great comfort in such a gloomy household." Elizabeth knew she was behaving childishly, but she could not seem to help herself. It was either that or weep.

A heavy silence fell in the carriage, broken only by the steady rustle of Elizabeth's pages turning and the tap of Peter's stick on the floor. Suddenly, he leaned forward and grasped her wrist.

Elizabeth was so startled that her book fell from her lap with a clatter. She clutched the penknife in her fist. To cover her confusion, she pulled her hand away and bent to retrieve the book.

"It will not be like that at Clifton anymore, Elizabeth," he said, his voice almost was it beseeching?

"Like what?" Elizabeth murmured, completely taken aback.

"As it was before you left. I was wrong, very wrong to have behaved as I did towards you. The quarrels, that business with the duke..."

Elizabeth held up her hand to stop the bewildering flow of his words. "Please. Let us never speak of that again."

"No. Of course." Peter sat back, and she could see the old coldness descend on him like a cloak. "I have no excuse. I was not myself when I returned from the Peninsula."

That Elizabeth could agree with wholeheartedly.

"But you have been gone a long time, Elizabeth," he continued. "Things have changed. I know that Clifton is not Venice."

Elizabeth snorted. That was an understatement if there ever was one.

Peter went on as if he had not heard her lapse in manners. "But I am certain you can be happy here again. I only wish to make amends to you."

Elizabeth was quite sick of men who felt they knew what was best for her, who thought they could order her life to suit themselves no matter what her own feelings were. "Oh, Peter." She sighed. "The only amends you could have made was to have left me to my own life and not have sent your flunky after me."

"Elizabeth, you are wrong about me. I am your brother—I want only what is best for you."

"You cannot even begin to know what that would be! Only I know what is best for me."

Peter merely shrugged. "We shall see." Then he added, very gently, "And you are also wrong about Nick Hollingsworth."

She was saved from answering when the carriage drew to a halt on the gravel drive curving in front of Clifton Manor. Elizabeth peered out from behind the wispy veil of her bonnet. The house had not changed at all, the grand Tudor façade with its incongruous pillared Georgian side wings, which had been added by her stepfather. It was a good deal tidier than when she had last seen it, however, and a bit less forbidding. The ivy was trimmed back, and the stone front steps gleamed beneath the feet of the servants assembled there.

Despite the polishing, the new flowers spilling from the beds, the crisp curtains behind the windows, the aura remained the same, a miasma of the living of so many generations. So much of her own past was there. The laughter of her beautiful mother, as she let her little daughter try on her gowns; her stepfather carrying her piggyback down the grand staircase; Peter dancing with her at her very first ball. There was also the dead duke. It was all there, waiting for her to take it back up again, as if no time had passed at all.

"Are you ready?" Peter asked. "They are waiting to greet you."

Shaken from her fancies, Elizabeth nodded and hastily tucked the book into her traveling case. "Yes, certainly."

Jenkins, the elderly butler who had been at Clifton since Elizabeth had come there as a child, was the first to step forward and welcome her as Peter assisted her from the carriage.

"Lady Elizabeth," Jenkins said. "May I say what a great honor it is to welcome you home again?"

The twinkle in his faded eyes belied his formal manner. Elizabeth smiled as she recalled how he had slipped her extra plum cakes at childhood teatimes. "Thank you, Jenkins," she answered. "It is very good to see you again."

"And Mrs. Smith is also quite eager to greet you," Peter added, indicating the black-clad, rosy-cheeked cook.

"Mrs. Smith!" Elizabeth cried in delight. "Do you still make that exquisite chocolate trifle?"

"I do, my lady, and there is some just waiting for your tea this afternoon."

Elizabeth kept her careful smile in place as she was introduced to a myriad of unfamiliar housemaids, kitchen maids, footmen, and gardeners. She had quite forgotten how very many people it took to run such a great house, after two years with only Bianca.

When they reached Daisy, and Elizabeth saw the tears shimmering in her lady's maid's eyes, her composure slipped, and all the tension of her long voyage melted. She forgot decorum and position entirely, and threw her arms around Daisy's small figure.

"My lady!" Daisy cried in shock.

"Oh, Daisy!" Elizabeth sobbed. "How I have missed you!"

"I missed you, too, my lady. I knew you would come home one day, so I never let that Lady Haversham entice me away, even when she wanted to send me to London with her daughter."

"You will never know how I wished you were with me in Italy. You would have adored it, after all those romances we read together! So many ruins and black-eyed counts." Disregarding propriety even further, Elizabeth took Daisy's arm and led her into the house, leaving Peter behind. She turned automatically toward the great staircase. "My rooms are ready?"

"Yes, my lady. I supervised the airing of them myself. It's just as you left it."

It was indeed. The pink silk curtains and bed hangings, the lace-skirted dressing table with its gilt Cupids cavorting around the mirror, even the porcelain doll (Martha) propped on the marble mantel, were all just as she remembered. Even the paintings on the walls, her own early efforts, had not been moved.

"Oh, Daisy, I would vow I was sixteen again!" Elizabeth removed her bonnet and sat down on the cushioned window seat that looked out at the gardens. "And the view is quite unchanged."

Daisy shooed away the maids who had already set to unpacking Elizabeth's trunk, and began to shake out the gowns herself. "Italy must have been ever so exciting, my lady."

"Oh, yes. Italy was Heaven."

Daisy held up the black velvet-and-satin gown Elizabeth had worn to the opera on that far-off night, when she had thought to entice Nicholas with its daring neckline. "And these were angel's robes, my lady?"

Elizabeth laughed. Now she remembered exactly why she had hired Daisy so long ago—her irreverence. "So they were! I wore gowns like that to operas, and balls, and breakfasts, and on gondola rides that lasted all night. And I saw art that only gods could have created. Art everywhere." She thought with a pang of the unrestored Veronese. "It was Heaven."

"Well, my lady," Daisy answered, briskly hanging the black gown up in the wardrobe. "Things can be lively around here, too."

"Yes?"

"Yes. Lady Haversham's poodles escaped and tried to eat some of the vicar's prize hydrangeas a month ago. Ever since then we have heard about nothing but greed and stealing in the Sunday sermons. And the Misses Allan just returned from wintering in Brighton, just bursting with all the gossip they heard there and eager to spread it about. It's almost Venice, without the art."

Elizabeth giggled helplessly. "Daisy, you always could lift me from my sulks! How is it you did not marry while I was away?"

"It was like this, my lady—no one asked me."

"Me, neither." Elizabeth sighed. "Except for Ottavio Tutino, but that does not count. He asks every lady to marry him when he is in his cups. We are better off not married, anyway, believe me."

It was Daisy's turn to giggle. "Oh, Lady Elizabeth, what people you met! But what shall you wear to supper? Jenkins says the vicar is coming to dine."

"Reverend Bridges? Oh, something very wicked I should think. Something to welcome myself home properly. What about that green velvet with the gold lace? And do be sure to tell Jenkins to have plenty of wine on hand. If I must listen to stories about prize hydrangeas, I will need it."

"My lady!" Daisy laughed.

Elizabeth looked back out at the garden, sunset pink now. "I know that everyone here is expecting a scandal now that I have returned—I may as well oblige them. I've nothing better to do."

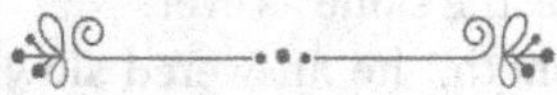

TWO HOURS LATER, a new woman from the travel-stained, weary waif emerged to greet the vicar in the Blue Drawing Room. She had missed supper, but had no intention of missing the vicar altogether.

She had exchanged her modest carriage dress for the green velvet and gold lace, which Bianca, in a fit of economizing, had created by modifying the Carnivale costume Elizabeth had worn the night she met Nicholas Hollingsworth. Her hair was swept up from her bared shoulders and held by golden ribbons; a faintly glistening powder had been dusted across the daring décolletage.

In the firelight of the drawing room she almost glittered, like a strange Italian painting dropped into the decorous manor.

She was not the pastel-clad miss that Mr. Bridges, the esteemed vicar of Clifton village, remembered from two years ago, who had stood quietly in the corners of assemblies, and always seemed to have paint streaks on her hands and clothes. His last view of her, cringing at her betrothal ball, was quite lost in this dashing lady. He gaped, and could scarcely contain his eagerness to rush out and spread the news among his parishioners.

Peter's lips thinned.

"Mr. Bridges!" Elizabeth cried gaily, holding her ungloved hand, her new sapphire ring sparkling on her ring finger, out to him. "How very long it has been, yet here you are, the same as ever."

"Lady Elizabeth," he answered slowly. "I must say *you* are not the same as ever."

"Am I not?" Elizabeth laughed merrily, trying to imitate Georgina at her most flirtatious. "It is this gown. I am far too old to don white in the evenings now." She wagged her finger playfully at the silent Peter. "Why, brother dear, are you not going to offer your sister something to drink? I vow I am still quite parched after that long journey!"

Peter bowed shortly. "There is ratafia, if you like, Elizabeth. Or I could ring for tea."

"Oh, pooh, no! Is that not brandy I see in your glass?"

"I hardly think—"

"I will have brandy. Thank you." Her voice was also new, steely with determination under a smile. Even

Peter took heed of the warning. He bowed again, and went to fetch her a brandy.

Elizabeth settled herself on a chaise by the fire, and smiled up at the vicar. "Now, Mr. Bridges, do sit beside me and tell me all the local news. I am quite perishing to hear if Miss Gray ever married her London viscount, and if Lady Haversham's daughters are all settled."

She whipped open her gold lace fan, and peered at the elderly vicar over its edge.

Lady Elizabeth Everdean had, quite momentously and dramatically, come home.

17

ELIZABETH WATCHED IN THE mirror as Daisy looped a long strand of pearls through her elaborate coiffure. She had remembered Derbyshire as quite lacking in social amenities, but in the weeks she had been back, they had attended several assemblies, dinners, musicales, and card parties. Many of the local families were in residence before departing for the London Season, and it was considered quite a social coup to have the odd and faintly scandalous Lady Elizabeth at their gatherings.

And Elizabeth had the distinct sense that Peter was trying, with a grim determination, to cheer her up by dragging her hither and yon, from tea party to dance, without a pause in between.

In her more dreamy schoolgirl days, when she had imagined an exciting Continental life, she would never have thought the fantastical, golden Venice would seem a solid reality and England a bizarre dream. Yet it had happened.

Clifton Manor, a beautiful house filled with fine furnishings, seemed an uncomfortable place, inhabited by the kind of people who should have been familiar but instead seemed to have strange ideas of what proper behavior should be. They were kind to her and always polite, to be sure, but she seemed not to be what they expected of their Lady Elizabeth, and they watched her closely to see what odd thing she would do next. She felt she was always on exhibit, like a tiger in a menagerie.

At night she would sometimes dream of floating free in a gondola, dappled in buttery sunlight while her handsome gondolier flirted with her in fluid Italian. She dreamed of rich wine on her tongue, almond cakes at Florian's, the scent of incense in the dim splendor of San Marco.

She would wake from these dreams sobbing with homesickness. The old stone church in the village, while lovely, couldn't rival the almost pagan splendor of a Byzantine cathedral. The servants looked quite scandalized when she drank more than a thimbleful of sherry before dinner, or wore one of her Italian gowns to a party.

Not that her life at Clifton Manor was bad in any way. The servants, despite their curiosity, were most happy to have a lady in residence again, even if she did nothing that was expected. Daisy adored the stories of the odd Venetian maid Bianca, and the narrow gray-pink house she had tended to so poorly. Daisy even posed for her own portrait, after an initial hesitation, and made over all Elizabeth's old pastel frocks by lowering the necklines and removing the excess furbelows. She even delighted in bringing in Georgina's letters on the morning trays of chocolate and toast.

Two footmen had cleaned out her old studio on the third floor, and Georgina had sent on all her works in progress. Elizabeth dutifully set up her easel, and even ground some pigments, but somehow, she could not paint. The brushes would just hang from her fingers, and the colors and images that used to flood her mind and make her forget all else refused to come to her. Her mind was a blank. Aside from the portrait of Daisy, she had not finished one work.

Even her appetite was gone. Mrs. Brown, the cook, tried to make her "Italian" meals, to no avail.

Elizabeth could not do anything but think of Nicholas, and the life she had left behind.

Every day, rain or sun, she would go walking through the fields and woods, striding along aimlessly. She hoped that if she could walk far enough, fast enough, she could leave him, the taste of him, the sound of his voice, far behind. She felt almost a physical pain in the pit of her stomach whenever she remembered his pale face revealing his betrayal.

She had loved him truly; indeed, she loved him still. Despite his lies, and the lie they had lived together for so many weeks. He lived in her heart, and he would not easily be dislodged. Even distance did not dim the memories.

One moment she would curse him, and vow that if she ever saw him again, she would spit in his face for leaving her to this, for lying to her and then never even writing to her. In the next instant, she would cry at the thought of never seeing his face again. It was like a never-ending "delicate time of the month." One night, unable to sleep, Elizabeth built up a fire in her bedroom grate and tried to feed all her sketches of him to the flames. She could not bring herself to do it. Instead, she brought out her hidden bottle of brandy, drank it, and cried until dawn.

All that came from that experiment was a raging headache. She had grown thinner, paler; she could see that now in the mirror. She knew that she could not go on in this stupid manner forever, but she didn't know how to stop it. She missed Nicholas; she missed Georgina and all their friends. She hated the fact that Peter set footmen to follow her wherever she went, hated sitting across from him at the dinner table, listening to his cool voice talk to her of inconsequential matters like the weather and the last gathering they had attended.

Most of all, she hated the Elizabeth she had become. The merry girl in Italy, so independent and confident in her abilities, would never have cried such a sea of tears. She would not have been so very indecisive over a mere man. Especially such a man, such a rake.

"Old Nick, indeed," she murmured, not realizing that she spoke aloud.

"I beg your pardon, my lady?" Daisy said.

"Oh, not a thing. I was merely thinking of a painting I am composing in my mind."

"Well, that is good that you are thinking of painting again! And what do you think of your hair, my lady?"

Elizabeth dutifully turned her head to examine the elaborate whorls and waves. "Exquisite, as always. You are more the artist than I am, Daisy. I am not so very certain about the gown, though."

"What is wrong with it, Lady Elizabeth?"

"I loathe white." She fluffed out the skirt of the silk and tulle gown, a creation left over from her days before she left. "It looks rather silly on a woman of nearly one-and-twenty! If only I had not already worn all my Italian gowns."

"White or not, it looks well on you, my lady. And you have your lovely Indian shawl to wear with it."

"Hmm, and quite appropriate for supper and cards at the Havershams'." Elizabeth dug under the dressing table for her discarded silk slippers. "I have half a mind to plead a megrim and stay home with a good book."

"I wouldn't want to do that, my lady. Not tonight, anyway."

"No? Why not?"

"I hear tell the Havershams have a new houseguest."

Elizabeth sighed. "Oh, lud! Not another pimply faced nephew, dangling for an heiress?"

"Oh, no, my lady." Daisy's voice dropped to a whisper. "I heard that this one is a sculptor. Newly arrived from Italy."

ELIZABETH STOOD in the doorway of the Havershams' grand drawing room, surveying the company assembled amidst the overstuffed, over-decorated chinoiserie that Lady Haversham was currently infatuated with. There were the Misses Allan, spinster sisters and arbiters of county morals, dressed in rusty black, and surveying everyone through their lorgnettes; the vicar, enjoying a very large glass of Madeira; Mr. Taylor, local eligible bachelor and heir to the Viscount Drake, dressed in the pink of London fashion and surrounded by giggling misses.

And conversing with their hostess was the person she sought—Sir Stephen Hampton, her old friend and one-time halfhearted suitor, looking just as she had last seen him in Venice.

He saw her as well, and gave a tiny nod in her direction. Elizabeth waved her white lace fan.

Peter took her arm in a firm grasp. "Shall we go in, my dear?" ·

Elizabeth did not look at him. "I suppose, since we are already here and have no hope of retreat."

The room hushed just a bit as they made their entrance, as it always did. Local society had grown accustomed to seeing the "odd" Lady Elizabeth, who had vanished from their midst so mysteriously two years ago, in company, but they were still wary of her. It was almost as if they expected her to sing bawdy songs at the pianoforte, or dance barefoot across their ballrooms.

She merely smiled and nodded as Peter escorted her to their hostess, and the hum of conversation slowly resumed.

"Ah, Lord Clifton, Lady Elizabeth," Lady Haversham cried, the feathers on her puce-and-lavender turban bobbing. "You must meet the newest addition to our little society, Sir Stephen Hampton. He is quite a renowned sculptor, and has only recently returned from Italy."

Peter raised a golden brow in Elizabeth's direction. "Italy? Indeed?"

"Yes," Lady Haversham replied. "I thought Lady Elizabeth would be particularly interested in meeting him. She was always so very artistic."

"Indeed I am very happy to meet him," answered Elizabeth. She held out her gloved hand for Stephen to bow over. "Your fame has quite preceded you, Sir Stephen. Even in the wilds of Cornwall, where I have lately lived."

"How do you do, Lady Elizabeth?" Stephen gave her hand the merest squeeze.

"Sir Stephen is on his way to begin a commission for the Duke of Ponsonby, for his late duchess's memorial," Lady Haversham interjected. "And speaking of marble, Lord Clifton, I do want to ask your opinion of the ruin I am thinking of having constructed in our park."

Lady Haversham led Peter away, leaving Elizabeth providentially alone with Stephen.

"Would you care for some refreshment, Lady Elizabeth?" he inquired politely.

"Oh, yes, thank you, Sir Stephen."

They did not speak again until they found a secluded alcove behind the refreshment table. Elizabeth threw her arms around his neck. "Oh, Stephen, you dear old thing! I have never in my life been so very happy to see anyone."

His arms tightened briefly. "Are you glad to see me, Elizabeth?"

"Terribly! I have missed you all so much." She sat down on the velvet bench, and smiled up at him. "Tell me, how is everyone, and what are you doing in Derbyshire?"

"Everyone is well. Georgina sent this on to you." He reached into his coat and withdrew a thick letter. "She has closed up your house in Venice, and I suspect you will see her here soon enough."

Elizabeth tucked the missive into her reticule, vowing to savor it later. "Oh, no! I have told her she must not think of coming here and leaving her work."

"I do not think she could have been stopped. Once your friend has set her mind to something it cannot be turned."

Elizabeth laughed, and tucked the precious letter

into her reticule, to be savored later, when she was alone. "No, that is true. Well, I shall be very happy to see her regardless."

"But how are you, Elizabeth? Are you well?"

"Me? Well enough. As you can see, Derbyshire is hardly Venice, but I am busy. There are dinners and musicales almost every evening."

"I thought you were in costume when I first saw you this evening!" He gestured toward her white gown.

"Oh, you mean this gown? I thought my black velvet not quite suited to the evening!" Elizabeth fluffed up her skirt, and smiled.

They were silent for a moment, listening to the Havershams' eldest daughter mangle a Mozart concerto on the pianoforte, then Stephen said, "You are not happy, Elizabeth."

She let her bright mask slip at last, and the comers of her mouth turned down. "No."

"You are not suited to this life."

"Not in the least! I miss my work desperately."

"I know how you can escape."

"Do you?" Elizabeth laughed mirthlessly. "Then pray tell me, Stephen. I have been racking my brain for a way for weeks."

He knelt beside her, and took her hand in his. "You could marry me."

18

IT WAS BY NO MEANS the most elegant brothel in London.

Smoke hung heavy in the air. The drink was watered, the green velvet upholstery and carpets were a bit shabby and threadbare, and the gilt of the mirrors' frames was chipped in spots. The "ladies" wore far too much paint, and the lace trim on their shifts was quite dingy (not that one could see that in the faint candlelight). Their faces were harsh, their laughter even harsher.

The patrons were scarcely any better-looking. These were not the dandies and the titled gentlemen who frequented Madame de Sevigny's establishment across town. These were low-level tradesmen, dock workers, sailors, smugglers. Baths were a rare occurrence for these men, and brawls frequent.

And the most disreputable sight in the entire room was Sir Nicholas Hollingsworth.

He was ostensibly involved in a game of cards, and winning, much to the chagrin of his odorous opponents. A half-empty bottle of cheap whiskey sat beside his pile of winnings; two of the house's finest, one blond and one a redhead, perched in his lap, one unfastening his shirt and the other giggling against his shoulder. He had refused to let any black-haired whores near.

“This is ever so dull, Nicky,” the redhead cooed. “You never take us upstairs anymore! Come on now, give us a chance.”

Nick threw back his head and laughed, reaching out to pinch the blonde's ample bum. "Maybe later, my loves. But right now..."

He was shocked from his inebriated haze when one of his opponents suddenly overturned the flimsy table, scattering cards, whiskey, and coins in every direction. The two whores fled, shrieking, leaving Nicholas sitting in the ruins, utterly stunned. He fumbled for the dagger hidden in his boot.

A slender fist grasped him by the shirtfront and pulled him unceremoniously to his feet. "I wouldn't go anywhere with those tarts if I were you," a voice, rough with smoke, said. "There is no telling what you could catch, Nicky."

Then Nicholas found himself looking down into the glittering green eyes of none other than Mrs. Georgina Beaumont.

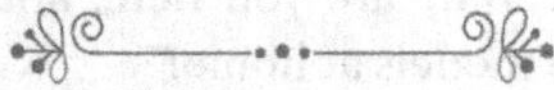

"PHEW! Have you never heard of a small invention called soap, Nicholas?" Georgina lit the only lamp to be found in Nicholas's lodgings. Her nose wrinkled as she surveyed the damage—clothes scattered on the floor, empty bottles, congealed plates of uneaten food. "There are also things called housemaids, though I doubt you could find one in desperate enough straits to clean this place."

"I don't want anyone here," he said pointedly. "I never see what it looks like here anyway."

"Yes, and that just shows how very low you've sunk. In Italy, you noticed everything and everyone about you," she said.

"Yes, I noticed how very stubborn lady artists can be." He sat down on a pile of dirty clothing and closed his eyes wearily.

"Oh, Nicholas," Georgina said sadly. "What have you done to yourself?"

"I have not done anything."

"Except drink and gamble and whore. I must say, you do not whore very well, either. You flirt and tease, but you never take a girl upstairs."

"You have only been following me for a week. I may have been engaged in all sorts of debaucheries before that."

"No. I doubt that you did anything differently at all before I found you." She paused sympathetically. "Poor Nicholas. None of them are Elizabeth, are they?"

"God's blood!" he exploded. "Why are you doing this, Georgina? Why are you here, and not sporting with the Italian models at home?"

Georgina blinked in shock at this deliberate cruelty. "That is unkind, Nicholas. And unfair. But since I know what pain you are in, I will overlook it. Once. And in answer to your question. I am here to shake some sense into you, you stupid man. And into Elizabeth, too."

"I like being unsensible, thank you very much, so you can just be on your way."

"Blast you! I saw the two of you in Italy. I know that you truly care for each other, love each other. Just as I loved my Jack, once upon a time. Probably you would be wed by now, if you had not turned out to be such a lying coxcomb." She pushed some dirty clothing off a chair and sat down gingerly. A piece of stationery crackled beneath her hip, and she pulled it out and read over the familiar handwriting with growing comprehension. "I see."

"See what?"

"This letter Lizzie gave you. You know what happened to her, then? Before she came to me in Italy? Her brother's beastly behavior, and the unfortunate demise of the duke."

He closed his eyes. "Yes. I know."

"So that is why you will not go to her, Nicholas? The truth gave you a disgust of her?"

"No! It is not that at all. Surely you know that nothing could give me a disgust of her, and certainly not the fact that she was horribly taken advantage of."

"Then what is it?" Georgina cried. "What could possibly be wrong?"

"She would not have me if I did go to her! You are completely right, I am a lying coxcomb. She deserves better than someone who would treat her as shamelessly as Peter and that duke dared to. She is better off as far from me as she can possibly go."

"Oh. Oh, Nicholas, what a terrible mess we have all made of things." Georgina went and. opened the window, leaning far out to breathe of the cool night air. "I have never seen two such stubborn, fatalistic people as you and Lizzie. You will not ever try to solve your differences, you just weep and get foxed, and declare that you are nobly letting her go on for a better life without you. Where is the man I knew in Venice?

You would never have let her get away from you there!"

"Georgina, it is not that easy."

"Pah! Of course it is. And you are just fortunate to have me as your friend. I will help you to resolve everything."

"Will you now?"

"Yes, I will. But you must cooperate."

"Cooperate. Yes. And just how do you propose to get Lizzie to forgive and forget all that I have done? Will you wave your magic wand?"

"Oh, very witty. Not that you deserve to know, but I am on my way to Derbyshire. I am leaving in the morning, and have a very fast phaeton to take me there. And you, Nicholas, will accompany me."

"Oh, will I?"

"Oh, you will. And please stop saying 'oh.'" She kicked disdainfully at an empty glass, and sent it rolling across the carpet. "The country air will do you some good, I think. Whatever would Lizzie say if she could see you living in this squalid manner?" Nicholas had the most bemused, dreamlike sensation of being completely overcome by a tidal wave.

His will was no longer his own. "She would probably say that it was no more than I deserve."

Georgina drummed her fingers on the windowsill thoughtfully. "No. Somehow I do not think that is what she would say at all. She would say—"

"M-MARRY YOU?" Elizabeth blinked up at Stephen.

"Why, yes." Stephen's face was quickly becoming quite as red as his hair. It was obvious that he was not at all accustomed to proposing to young ladies, or to having his proposals greeted with obvious shock and dismay. "It is the perfect solution to your difficulties. If you ran away to Gretna Green with me tonight, you would no longer be under your stepbrother's guardianship. You could resume your painting, return to your home in Italy, whatever you like. I would not make, er, um, *husbandly* demands upon you, I vow that on my honor."

It was quite the longest speech Elizabeth had ever heard him make. She felt the tickle of tears on her eyelashes, and turned away to fumble for a handkerchief. "Oh, Stephen, I do seem to have become such a watering pot since I returned to England! You are quite the sweetest man I have ever met, and I am truly blessed to have you for my friend."

He smiled grimly. "But you are refusing me."

"I must. I think it is the only sane thing to do. Do not think I'm not tempted by your offer, because I am, terribly. I quite long for the Italian sun on my face again."

"Then why not accept me? We enjoy the same things in life; we have the same friends. I could give you a comfortable home. We could be content together."

"Content, yes." Elizabeth had a sudden vision of the two of them, doddering old artists wielding brushes and palette knives in their palsied hands, never speaking to each other because there was no need. She almost laughed. "But never truly happy. I had a truly happy day once, and I know how that can be. I could never ruin your life by depriving you of the chance to find that; that would be poor repayment indeed for your friendship."

"Is it your secretary, then? Nicholas?"

She felt the tears beginning in earnest, and ducked her head into the lace ruffles of her bodice. "I did love Nicholas once, yes. In point of fact, I strongly suspect I love him still."

"Then—"

"No! It is of no use to even speak of it. I do not even know where he is, and if I knew I am not sure what I would do about it."

They sat together quietly, listening to Miss Haversham finish off Mozart and a Miss Julian begin a Handel sonata. Finally, Stephen took her hand in his very gently.

"Are you certain I cannot persuade you?" he said.

"Quite, quite certain."

"Then, dear friend, I hope you will still call for me if ever you require assistance." Then he pressed a kiss to her fingers and left her, winding his way through the milling crowd to take leave of their hostess.

Elizabeth dabbed at her eyes and smoothed her skirts. She very much wanted her own fireside and a glass of brandy, but unfortunately a tedious evening still stretched endlessly before her.

"If only I could hide here in this alcove all night," she mused aloud.

"That would be insufferably rude," Peter said from beside her.

Elizabeth spun around. "Really, Peter! Must you creep up on me so?"

"I was merely coming to tell you that Lady Haversham requires a fourth at her whist table."

"You know I dislike whist." Elizabeth hated the querulous tone of her voice, but she. couldn't seem to help herself. It had really been a most trying evening, and her head ached. The façade had become so heavy.

Peter observed her flushed cheeks and over-bright eyes through his quizzing glass. "You and that sculptor were having a most involved discussion, my dear."

"Yes, we were. Fellow artists are quite rare in Derbyshire, you know."

"And perhaps you knew him before? In Italy?"

Elizabeth's frayed temper snapped. "If I did, it is hardly any of your affair! And now, if you have no objections, I must join our kind hostess." She wrapped her Indian shawl over her shoulders and turned her back on him, stalking away across the drawing room in obvious high dudgeon.

19

THE NEXT DAY, ELIZABETH went for a very long walk. She ended up on her favorite seat, a large, flat rock atop the crest of a hill, placed fortuitously in the shade of a tall oak. From this vantage point she could see the house and fields of Clifton Manor spread out before her.

It was a lovely, peaceful place in which to be alone to think. She had quite forgotten how beautiful England could be when one was solitary in its cool, green prettiness.

And she had a great to deal to think of. Such as Stephen's surprising appearance in Derbyshire, and his even more surprising proposal of marriage. It would have been a most convenient solution, to marry him and resume her career. With such a successful sculptor as her husband, she could even attract more patrons, have the possibility of joining more professional societies.

If only she loved him, or even felt more than a sisterly fondness for him. But he could not make her laugh until her ribs ached; he did not make her very toes curl with just the thought of one of his kisses. The only time he had kissed her, once in

Rome, it had been distinctly lacking in finesse and passion.

Unlike Nicholas's kisses.

"I do miss you, Nicholas," she whispered. "Was I wrong to go away from you?"

She had been plagued by doubts all through the sleepless night. Did she give in to Peter's demands too easily? Should she have given Nicholas a greater chance to explain his actions?

But what explanations were there? He had lied to her for weeks, about his feelings, his very identity.

"Just as you lied to him, you foolish girl," she said aloud, her voice thick with bitterness at that flash of self-realization. She had lied to him, as he had to her, for their entire acquaintance.

"Talking to yourself, Elizabeth?"

Elizabeth looked up with a gasp to see Peter leaning negligently against the tree. He was dressed for riding, and his horse was tethered nearby.

She had been far too preoccupied with her musings to even hear his approach.

"You are always creeping up on me so!" she answered. "And, no, I was not speaking to myself, I was talking to that sheep over there."

"Hmm. May I join you, then, or is this a private moment for you and the sheep?"

She hesitated, then nodded and slid over to make a space on the rock.

"Lady Haversham tells me she asked you if you would paint her portrait," he commented, as he took the proffered seat.

"Yes. We spoke of it last night over the whist table. She wants a new portrait to present to Lord Haversham on their anniversary."

"Will you accept?"

"I don't know. Perhaps. I am rather out of practice."

"I think it would be a very good thing for you to work, perhaps lift you out of these doldrums."

She laughed shortly. "I was working, until I came here."

A heavy silence fell, broken only when Peter said, "Would you care to go to Town for the Season?"

Elizabeth blinked, certain she had not heard correctly. "London?"

"Yes. That is the only Town I know that will be commencing its Season soon. I received an invitation to Lady Ponsonby's ball."

"But you detest London."

Peter shrugged. "*Detest* is surely too strong a word. I prefer the country, certainly, but I have been spending more time in Town of late. It has many diversions I am sure you would enjoy—balls, theater, lectures, museums, and galleries."

Elizabeth's eyes narrowed. "Why? Is there someone there you wish to betroth me to? Some ancient duke or marquis?"

Peter clicked his tongue. "How very suspicious you have become! I merely thought you might enjoy a broader society. You may even secure some commissions. London is certainly full of people who have nothing better to do with their time than sit about having their portrait painted."

Elizabeth was still suspicious. London did sound tempting, full of more of the amenities of civilization that she had come to enjoy while on the Continent. And she could seek out new patrons, as Peter had said, try to build a new career. If only she were certain of Peter's motives.

"Perhaps," was all she said.

"Elizabeth," Peter said slowly, "I do not want you to be unhappy, as I see you have been."

"I am not unhappy. Merely at loose ends."

"Nonetheless, I want you to feel as if Clifton were your true home. I also wish you could forgive me."

"Forgive you?"

"Yes. You were fond of me once; could we not try to rebuild something of that?"

She rose to her feet, almost shaking with disbelief. "Peter, you treated me shockingly when you came home from the Peninsula. You forced me to become engaged against my wishes. Then, when I had found a life, a happiness of my own, you snatched it away."

"Elizabeth, be reasonable."

"No! You men, you think you can do the most outrageous things and we will just forgive you, smile, and go on as if nothing had happened. Well, no. It does not work this time. It simply cannot."

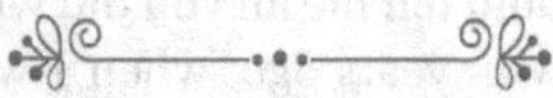

"THIS CANNOT GO ON!"

Elizabeth didn't even look up from the sketchbook she had propped up beside her plate of toast and marmalade, though inside she was thoroughly shocked. In the days since their scene on the hillside, Peter had never burst out in such a fashion, or even spoken to her of anything but the weather. Their meals had been silent, her days in the studio solitary. Elizabeth had even begun to bring her drawing to the table.

Apparently, this breakfast was to be different. "Cannot what?" she asked quietly.

"You know what I am talking about, so do not insult my intelligence by pretending otherwise."

Peter threw his crumpled napkin down beside his untouched plate. "I am speaking of this spoiled, childish attitude you have been exhibiting since I asked if you cared to go to Town."

"Spoiled! Childish?" Elizabeth dropped her pencil and exchanged glare for glare along the polished length of the table.

"Yes. You drift about like a wraith in some bad novel, walking the fields all hours of the day. When we do go out, you insist on shocking everyone with your language and your gowns. You are even refusing to show basic table manners and converse politely at breakfast."

Elizabeth could only gape at him, astonished. Where had her cool, distant stepbrother vanished to?

"You used to speak with me at breakfast," he continued. "You would tell me all you did with your days."

"That that was years ago, when I was just a prattling girl. Much has happened since then, and I prefer quiet in the mornings. And, in point of fact, *you* are the one who has been lacking in conversation these past days."

He had the grace to blush a little at the reminder of all that had happened since the days she would chatter through all their meals. He held up a sheaf of invitations for her perusal. "Then if you are so unhappy in this house, why not come to London? We have already been invited to many routs there."

Elizabeth snorted. "I do not feel in the least like being gaped at, at balls and card parties more than I already am! If I go to Town, it will be on my terms, and not to go to parties at the Havershams' town house, as if we were still here." She could feel her face turning scarlet, could feel all her loneliness, her anger at the men in her life, rushing up to the surface from the place she had so carefully pushed it down to.

"And," she continued, "if you wish to talk about childish behavior, let us talk about *you*. Because I refused to live my life according to your dictates, you chased me down. No, worse, you sent a spy after me. You took me away from my friends, my work, and to what purpose? To have your own way? That is childish, not to mention morally reprehensible, Peter Everdean."

Her temper at last spent, Elizabeth was utterly mortified to feel tears spilling onto her cheeks. She gathered her sketches up in her arms, and turned away. "Now, if you will excuse me..."

"Elizabeth," Peter called out softly, "please wait."

She paused with her hand on the door, but did not turn back. "What is it?"

"I did not bring you to England for some petty revenge, though it may have seemed so to you. And even to myself."

"No? Then what was the reason?"

"I wanted to make amends toward you for my beastly behavior after I returned from Spain. I needed to make you understand that I..." He broke off, his own eyes suspiciously bright.

Peter, crying? Elizabeth was utterly bewildered. "To make me understand what?" she asked, her voice gentle. He was seeming more like the brother she recalled from years ago, the brother she had thought long dead. "Tell me, please, Peter. I feel so overturned by this whole affair, but I want so desperately to understand."

"Come with me," he said, pushing back his chair. "I want to show you something."

Elizabeth followed him to the library, the one room where she was never allowed, and watched with wary eyes as he unlocked the bottom drawer of his desk. She saw the flat case that held her own miniature, the one painted on her fifteenth birthday, which Peter had carried with him to Spain. She also saw another box, which he removed from the drawer.

"Come and look," he said, opening the box and carefully laying out a bundle of ribbon-tied letters, another miniature portrait, a dried gardenia, and a woman's ruby earring. "Here are all my secrets for your perusal, Lizzie."

Still unsure, she reached for the miniature, cradling it in the palm of her hand as she examined the portrait painted on the ivory.

It was a girl, a woman, of great beauty. Elizabeth's artist's eye instantly envied her high cheekbones, her delicate jaw and high cheekbones. The pale oval of her face was crowned by a heavy mass of black hair; her dark eyes seemed to flash and laugh. Swinging from her ears, peeking from loops of her dark hair, were the ruby earrings. "She is very lovely," Elizabeth managed to say at last.

"You look very like her."

She looked down again at the dark lady, and shook her head. "No. We both have dark hair, but my face is much rounder than hers. She is so much more exotic than I ever could be."

"I thought, when I returned from the war, that you resembled her very much indeed. In some of my less lucid moments I thought you *were* her. And I took my rage out on you, since she was beyond me forever." He fell silent, twirling the earring absently through his long fingers. "When you fled under those horrible circumstances, I was shaken to my senses. I longed to tell you, to tell you how much I loathed myself for what I had done. I wanted to make amends to you, but you were not here to listen to my apologies. For two years I lived with the knowledge that I had failed you, after our parents entrusted you to my care." He looked up at last into her pensive face. "Lizzie, my dear sister, can you ever forgive me? For everything? It is no excuse, I know, but I was not myself."

Elizabeth did not answer. Instead, she held out the painting. "Who was she?"

An odd half smile curled at his lips. "Carmen. She was a wealthy widow from Seville, but she worked with the partisans against Napoleon. She was a spy for us, until she betrayed us to the French, and your Nicholas was almost killed in the resulting battle. She died, as well." Peter tossed the miniature back into its box. "She was also my wife."

ALONE AT LAST in her bedroom, Elizabeth stretched out on her bed to turn Peter's words over and over in her mind. Her entire world had tilted yet again, and she couldn't yet hold on to the idea that Peter was not exactly the villain she had thought him to be for so long. He was not yet her beloved brother again, either. She was not certain what he was.

Except that he was a widower.

"Another love gone awry," she murmured. "Can love never be right in this family?"

For the first time since coming back to Clifton Manor, she remembered the utter magic of her time with Nicholas, untainted by what had come after. She remembered lazy luncheons at Florian's, boat rides in sunshine and starlight that she had never wanted to end. She remembered how they would laugh together, how interested he had been in her work, how they had kissed. She even remembered how he would trail after her in galleries and churches, trying not to yawn and whispering delicious *bon mots* into her ear to make her giggle.

She remembered that the sound of his laughter was the only thing in all the world that could rival the joy of a blank canvas and a palette full of paint. She also remembered the portrait, hidden away in her studio, that she had begun that sunny day in the Italian countryside. The portrait she had never wanted to see again.

Barefoot, she padded up the stairs to her studio and searched through the carefully crated canvases Georgina had sent her until she found the one she wanted. She propped it on an empty easel and stepped back to study it.

There, with vineyards and their white villa in the background, was her Nicholas. Not the Old Nick of the scandalmongers, or the Captain Hollingsworth of Peter's regiment, but Nicholas. His shirt was open at his throat, baring a delicious V of golden skin and the merest hint of dark, curling hair; his black hair was tousled in the wind. He was laughing at her, the laughter she had always smiled foolishly at hearing. None of that had been a lie.

She did love him. Her heart had not been whole

since the day she left him. She needed him as she needed air, water, and art. It was not a choice. And now she saw that she had been a fool to tum her back on that love, even if she had been so angry.

Peter's stories of life in Spain, which he had spun for her into the small hours of the night, had made her begin to see what had made Nicholas go to Italy in the first place. Nicholas owed Peter his life.

So, in a fashion, Elizabeth owed Peter her life, as well.

She went back to her room, and took out writing paper and pencil from her desk. After an hour of contemplative nail-biting, she began:

"My dearest Nicholas..."

She labored over that letter all night, crossing out lines, trying to sound forgiving and friendly, but not so very forgiving that she became maudlin.

It was a very difficult task, and the fire burned merrily with discards before she at last had a version she was content with. She addressed it to the lodgings she had found among Peter's papers, sealed it and promptly lost all her nerve. She stuck it hastily into a drawer amid her silk stockings, and went to bed to sleep and try to forget her folly.

Nicholas was probably far away from England by now. And he more than likely did not remember her or what they had shared. It had been too long, and she had been too silent.

And, after all, what chance could there really be for them, after all that had happened?

20

"SEE, I TOLD YOU THAT country air was exactly what you needed." Georgina smiled at Nicholas over the rim of her teacup. "Your eyes are much clearer already."

"That is because there is no proper tavern in this entire blighted village. And this place only serves watered ale." He indicated the small public room of the Dog and Duck Inn, where he had taken rooms and where Georgina had come to join him for a late breakfast. She, however, was comfortably ensconced in a friend's country manor for the duration of their stay.

"Well," she answered, "the house where I am staying boasts an excellent cellar and a fine chef. I'm sure Lady Overton would not mind in the least if you and Elizabeth were to come to supper some evening soon."

"If we ever actually meet with Elizabeth. I think Peter must have her cloistered in that house."

"Not at all. I have heard that she is out and about quite a great deal. And we shall see her very soon, I am sure. We must be careful, and approach her when she is away from that horrid stepbrother of hers. I do not want to cause her any more trouble. In point of fact, I have often wondered if I did her more harm than good when I took her in two years ago." Georgina set her cup aside and lowered the veil of her fashionable hat. "But that is all past. I am taking tea this afternoon with a woman named Haversham, and I am quite hoping Elizabeth will be there. Care to escort me?"

Nicholas shuddered. "Tea with someone named Haversham? No, I thank you. Besides, I am not at all certain Elizabeth has forgiven me, or even begun to think of me in a more kindly fashion. She might very well flee in horror if she saw me at the tea table with no warning whatsoever."

"Hmm, yes, quite right. But you will attend the assembly tomorrow evening with me?"

"I shall certainly try. I have no previous engagements, I believe."

"Ha ha."

"In the meantime, Georgina, do behave yourself. We are meant to be inconspicuous, remember?"

"Of course!" Then she stood, shook out her purple-and-gold-striped walking dress, unfurled her ruffled purple parasol, and swept out, amid the stares of every person in the room. "I shall see you this afternoon, Nicholas!"

"Inconspicuous, indeed," Nicholas murmured. The thought of having that woman as a *de facto* sister-in-law for the rest of his days was indeed a daunting one—but not enough to keep him from begging Elizabeth on hands and knees to marry him.

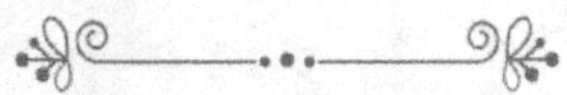

DAISY HUMMED as she tidied Elizabeth's bedroom, even sang a bit as she hung freshly pressed gowns in the wardrobe and laid bonnets away in their boxes. It was a lovely spring day, and Clifton Manor seemed quite bright and fragrant since Elizabeth had emerged from her cocoon and taken an interest in the housekeeping—and in painting.

All the servants, even the tweenie, had sat for sketches, which Daisy now gathered up and put away in a portfolio. Work seemed easier, somehow, when artistic endeavors broke up the monotony of dusting and polishing.

Even the earl smiled, laughed sometimes even, and went walking with his sister in the gardens after supper. There was talk of a grand ball to be held at Clifton Manor, of a trip to London.

Daisy sang out again as she opened one of the dressing table drawers and started to straighten the tangle of stockings there. A sealed letter fell from a knot of pale pink silk.

"Oh, no!" Daisy picked up the square of vellum and squinted down at the scrawled direction. "Lady Elizabeth must have forgotten to post this."

She considered taking it up to the studio where Elizabeth was working, but then shrugged and slipped it into her apron pocket. She was going into the village to buy some ribbon, anyway; she would simply post it while she was there.

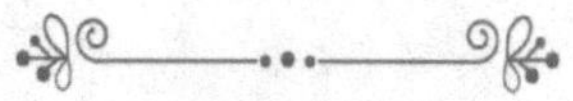

Nicholas stood for a very long time outside the Dog and Duck, attracting many a curious stare from the passersby, who were not accustomed to gentlemen dressed in quite that height of fashion standing about on the streets. He heard the whispered speculations on the style of his cravat, and his silver walking stick, and most of all from young ladies, his "romantic" air of "melancholy."

One brave soul even asked him outright if he was Lord Byron "in disguise."

Nicholas simply observed. He watched the people who passed him—shopkeepers and farmers and nannies with their charges, even one grand lady in her carriage. He had never lived in the country; he was very much a product of London, with its soot and its excesses. And the sunbaked hamlets he had seen in Spain in no way resembled this place, full of Tudor architecture and muddy streets.

Somehow he could not envision Elizabeth ensconced here, amid all this Englishness. He could not see her gossiping over bolts of muslin at the draper's, or taking tea with these silly young girls who giggled at him from the tiny tea shop across the way.

His love belonged under sunnier skies than these, with paint under her nails, plenty of champagne to drink, and lots of artists to chatter with at parties.

"Oh, Elizabeth," he murmured. "I should have snatched you up and run very far away with you when I had the opportunity. I should have taken you off and made you marry me, despite what you said."

Too late, his conscience chided. You were a complete fool and now you are paying the price.

So deep in his own thoughts was Nicholas that he

did not even see the cloaked young woman scurrying along the walkway until she had collided with him and sent them both tumbling to the ground. Papers and ribbons flew from the woman's basket.

Nicholas immediately sprang to his feet and held out a hand to assist her, brushing ineffectually at the dirt on her dark-colored cloak. "I do beg your pardon, miss! So very clumsy of me."

"Oh, no, not at all, sir!" she answered breathlessly. "It was my fault. I was in such a hurry to catch the post." She stuffed the papers back into the basket, gave him a merry smile, and hurried on her way. "Thank you, sir! Good day to you!" she called back over her shoulder.

"Good day," Nicholas said to her retreating back.

That was the most excitement he could expect of the day.

As he bent to retrieve his hat, he glimpsed one of the girl's letters, stepped on and half covered with mud. He started to shout after her, but she was out of his sight. Then he held the letter up and read the direction: "Sir Nicholas Hollingsworth."

"OH, WHERE CAN IT BE!" Elizabeth overturned the drawer onto the carpet, tossing stockings every which way in her frantic search.

The letter was nowhere to be found, even after she had turned every sheer bit of silk inside out.

"My lady? Are you lookin' for somethin'?"

Elizabeth glanced up to see Ellie, one of the junior housemaids, watching her curiously from the doorway. "Yes," she answered, and brushed a stray stocking from her head. "A letter. I seem to have misplaced it."

"Oh, Daisy must have it, my lady. She went to the village not half an hour ago to post the letters and fetch some ribbon."

"Post them!" Elizabeth wailed. "Oh, no! She can't!"

She was utterly aghast that everything that was in that blighted letter, all the love and longing she had poured out from her pen, was now floating free in the world. She was especially aghast that Nicholas might actually receive the letter and read it.

She did love him, yes. She was even rather close to understanding what he had done. But that did not mean that she was ready for him to know that!

"This is terrible."

Ellie watched in bewilderment as her mistress ran past her, down the staircase, and out the front door, slamming it loudly behind her.

Elizabeth hurried across the damp lawn and down the road that led to the village, clad only in an old yellow muslin round gown she wore for painting and thin kid slippers, her hair falling from the ribbon she had tried to catch it up in.

She was almost halfway to the village, a cramp forming in her side, when she saw him. Standing by a hedgerow, watching her run toward him.

"No," she gasped. "You are just a dream."

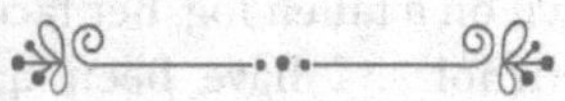

NICHOLAS KNEW that he had never seen anything more beautiful in all his pitiful life than Elizabeth Everdean running across a country lane.

She was hardly a graceful runner, moving at a painful, gasping gait. Her black hair had half tumbled from its ribbon, and her hem was muddied.

Yet no Incomparable, no Diamond of the First Water, could compare. He had tried to forget her in his wild ways since they had parted so painfully in Venice. Now he knew that he could never have possibly forgotten her, if he had caroused for a century.

"No," he said. "I am not a dream."

She moved slowly closer, so close that he could smell her lilies-of-the-valley perfume. "Then why are you here, Nicholas? Rusticating?"

He smiled at her crookedly. "My dear, you know me better than that. I am only here in this wilderness because of you."

"Me?"

"Yes. I have been a week at the Dog and Duck, all because of you."

"An entire week?" She looked up at him, her eyes wide and astonished. "In the village? Why did you not come to Clifton Manor, to call on me?"

"I was afraid you would have thrown me out on my ear."

Her lips thinned. "And so I would have, you rogue!"

He held out her crumpled and stained letter. "Would you truly, Elizabeth?"

She sat down on a fallen log, her face buried in her hands. "Oh, Nicholas. I have been quite desperate these past weeks."

"Oh, my dear, I..."

"Shh," she interrupted. "I do love you. The time we had together in Venice was everything I wanted in life. But I am not certain that we can have that again. That we can come to trust again."

Nicholas sat beside her, his knee barely brushing her skirts, but not daring to touch her in any other way. "I cannot blame you, Elizabeth. You have been through so very much already, and what I did was unforgivable."

"You lived a lie with me for weeks, Nicholas."

"Yes. I felt I had no other choice. Your letter says that Peter told you of what happened in Spain, so you do know what I owe him. And finding you was all he asked of me, even if I could not fulfill my promise to him."

"You could have told me! I might have railed at you at first, but I would have come to understand. You know that I am far from being a saint. I have made mistakes in my life, too, horrible ones. We could have helped each other."

"I know that, my love. Now I can do everything just as I should have done it. But then I was too scared."

"Scared? Of what?"

"Of you, of course."

Elizabeth snorted in disbelief. "Me?"

"That is a very bad habit you have gotten into, Elizabeth, and yes. I was scared of you, of what you would do. I was in love with you almost from the first moment I saw you, and I could not give that up. I did not want you to look at me with anger and disappointment, as you did that last day. I kept putting off the inevitable—because being with you made me happier than I ever thought anyone could be. Because I love you, Elizabeth."

She turned her face from him, and his heart sank. He thought she was disgusted with him, with his professions of love. Then he saw her shoulders trembling. Slowly, still wary of rejection, he put his hands on her shoulders and turned her back to him. She was crying, perfect, precious, diamondlike tears that glistened in her eyelashes and on her cheeks. She grabbed him by the collar of his coat and pulled him down to her.

"You utter idiot," she whispered. "I love you, too."

Then, much to Nicholas's shock and delight, she kissed him.

ELIZABETH WAS a bit shocked herself at her hoydenish behavior. The shock was quite buried, however, beneath her delight at having her lips on Nicholas's again.

It was every bit as wondrous as she remembered. Finally, so dizzy she feared she might swoon, she drew back and gently touched his cheek. "You never wrote to me."

"You told me not to," he answered, his voice deeper than usual, his eyelids slumberous.

"And you believed me?" She laid her cheek against his shoulder, and breathed deeply of his evergreen soap scent. "I have been aching to know what you were doing all these weeks."

Nicholas almost blushed. "Pining for you, my love, of course. What were you doing?"

"Oh, ever so many fascinating things." Elizabeth thought of whist at the Havershams', where she was meant to be taking tea right that moment, carriage rides with the Misses Allan—and Stephen's proposal. "Well, you must tell me of all of them across our breakfast table when we are married."

Elizabeth sat straight up. "Married!"

"Yes. I want you to be my wife, Elizabeth."

"I never said I would marry you, Old Nick Hollingsworth."

"Madam! Are you offering me *carte blanche*? I am shocked."

"Oh! You... you popinjay!" Elizabeth stood and turned her back to him. "How can I marry you? You have not even asked me yet. Properly, on your knees."

She glanced back over her shoulder to find him kneeling at her feet. She laughed aloud at the comic sight he made, mud covering his fine trousers and polished boots. "Whatever are you doing, Nicholas?"

"Kneeling, of course. Or is this better?" He fell face forward into the mud. "I am completely prostrate before you, Lady Elizabeth. Please marry me. I am quite desperately in love with you."

Elizabeth laughed even harder, so hard that she fell over beside him in the mud and muck. "How could I say no to such a gallant proposal? Yes. I will marry you."

"Dearest!" Nicholas attempted to plant a muddy kiss on her lips, but she held him off.

"I am still angry with you, you know," she said. "I feel I must tell you that right now. You hurt me terribly, and it will take many years for you to make amends to me. Perhaps even an entire lifetime."

"What if I were to begin making the amends right this moment?" He began softly kissing her neck.

"I would say you are doing an excellent job of it thus far."

"I can do even better."

"Oh, yes?"

His dark eyes were serious as he looked down at her. "I can take you back to Italy."

Her smile froze. "Italy?"

"Yes. If that is what you want. Or we could go to India, or China, or Canada. Anywhere you want, that is where we will go."

"You would do that? Give up your place in London society simply so your wife could paint and cause a scandal on the Continent?"

"My entire life has been a scandal, my dear. What could one more be? For you, I would live in a hut in Siberia. I would walk across Egypt, take up residence in a Cairo tomb. You want to be in Italy, I can see it in your eyes when I speak of it. I would be a brute indeed to keep you here, and deprive the world of your talent." He traced a thumb across her mud-streaked cheek. "And perhaps once we are in the sun again the color will come back to your cheeks."

Elizabeth threw herself against him, her tears wet on both their cheeks. "It will, I know it! Once away from Lady Haversham, I will bloom like a veritable garden. We will be happy in Italy... or anywhere, as long as we have each other."

Nicholas clung to her like a drowning man, his face buried in her black hair. "Even if you are angry with me still?"

"Even so." She kissed him again, and then again. "I love you enough, Nicholas Hollingsworth, to overcome anything."

"Then I should marry you very soon, before you lose this conviction."

"Yes, you should." She leaned against him, happily contemplating things she had never thought of seriously before-things like wedding gowns and baby rattles. "Shall we marry here, or in Italy?"

"Wherever you like, as long as you say 'I do.' "

"Here, then. I don't want to give you time to change your mind, though I have so shocked poor Mr. Bridges that he may refuse to perform the ceremony. And then..." She stopped, blushing an absolute crimson.

"Then what?"

"Then what of, um, babies?"

Nicholas laughed. "I like babies. Do you?"

"Sometimes. If he has your dark eyes."

"Oh, no, no. She will have your gray eyes, and your wondrous smile."

Elizabeth couldn't help but smile that wondrous smile. "So she will. And she will be quite gifted, I'm sure—she will be painting landscapes at age three."

"Two!"

"Perhaps she will even be born with a paintbrush in her hand, so she can start right away."

"My love." Nicholas pressed a kiss against her hair. "I am sure of it."

"There is just one thing you have to do before we can marry, go to Italy, and have this gifted, gray-eyed daughter."

"Oh? And what is that?"

"You must ask Peter's permission."

21

ELIZABETH SQUEEZED HER EYES tightly shut, trying not to wriggle about as Georgina, Daisy, and a fleet of housemaids fluttered around her. "Can I not look now?" she said.

"Not yet!" Georgina admonished. "Just one moment more."

Elizabeth could hear the rustle of satin, could smell tulle and roses. She twisted impatiently. "Georgie! Hurry. We will be late."

"My dear, they can hardly begin without you. But you may look now."

Georgina's hands turned her toward the mirror, and she slowly opened her eyes.

"No," she breathed. "That is not me."

"Oh, I assure you that it is!" Georgina laughed. A vision was reflected in the glass, an ethereal vision. The gown, newly arrived from London, was a soft sea of palest blue-green silk. The tulle overskirt was sewn with tiny pearls and crystals in the form of roses and lilies. The satin slippers peeping from the hem were sewn with the same beadwork.

The vision's hair was a loose river of black, caught up with a wreath of white roses. Perfectly matched pearls, her betrothal gift from Peter, gleamed in her ears and about her throat.

"You are the most beautiful bride," Georgina said. Tears shimmered on her cheeks.

"As beautiful as you, when you married Jack?"

"Oh, ever so much more beautiful! I wore a rumpled carriage dress over the anvil at Gretna Green." Georgina dried her eyes, and turned to pick up a nosegay of roses that matched the hair wreath. "Here are your flowers, Lizzie."

"I picked them from the garden just this morning, Lady Elizabeth," said Daisy.

Elizabeth inhaled deeply of their sweet, early summer scent. "They are perfect. This is a perfect day."

"And it has only just started!" Georgina checked her own reflection in the mirror, straightening her feathered hat and smoothing the bodice of her pale-yellow silk gown. "It can only grow more perfect as it goes on. Such as when you see Nicholas waiting for you at the church."

Elizabeth giggled into her flowers.

A knock sounded at the door. "Elizabeth?" Peter called. "Are you quite ready? The carriage is waiting."

"Come in, Peter," she answered.

Peter entered the room impatiently, shaking his watch by its gold chain, but halted abruptly at the sight of his sister standing there.

"Elizabeth," he said softly. "You are the very image of your mother."

Elizabeth smiled. She was not a bit like the blond Isobel, even in her stunning new gown, but it was a very nice thing to hear. It seemed to bring her mother closer to her on this most important day. "Thank you, Peter. And you look very like your father, even that waistcoat you are wearing. I have never seen you wear red brocade before!"

"It is a festive day, is it not? A time for new beginnings. Ivory satin just didn't seem appropriate." He took her arm and slowly, as if afraid she would pull back, kissed her cheek. "If my father were here, he would be filled with pride at the thought of escorting you down the aisle. I hope that you will accept me in his stead."

"I would be delighted if you would give me away." She gave him a small, ironic smile. "After all, if it were not for you, Peter, I would never have met Nicholas, and this day could never have happened."

"Touché," he said, with an answering smile. "I know that you are not certain of your feelings toward me, Elizabeth."

"Peter, I—"

"No, please, let me finish. I know that I have a great deal of work in my future to make you forgive me completely, for us to make a new sort of friendship. But I do love you, Lizzie. I want to be your brother again, if you will allow me to."

"I want that, as well," Elizabeth answered slowly. "I cannot say that the past will be fully forgotten. But, God willing, the future will be a long one, and we will have many new roads to travel together. And my children will have great need of their uncle."

He lifted her hand to his lips and kissed it. "Thank you. I vow that I will never cause you to doubt me again."

"I do believe you. Now, we should not keep the vicar waiting."

"No. We have a wedding to attend."

THE STONE NORMAN church in the village was full, every pew taken and a few unfortunate latecomers standing at the back. Lady Haversham, her poodles, and all her pink-lace-clad daughters had claimed one pew all for themselves. The Misses Allan had left off their black just for the occasion and wore dark green.

On the bride's side of the church, a flurry of artists from Italy and London and Paris were seated in a sea of bright colors, laughing and gossiping and finding out who had gained what plum commission. Yet even they fell silent as the organ swelled with the processional, and Georgina swept down the aisle with her bridesmaid's nosegay held elegantly before her.

Then Elizabeth appeared, her fingers clutching Peter's arm, her eyes only on her bridegroom, unhindered by a veil.

Nicholas was the most handsome she had ever seen him, in his blue coat, his smile wide and white as he watched her come to him, as he took her hand in his, and kissed her cheek much to the disapproval of the vicar.

Then Mr. Bridges intoned, "Dearly beloved..." And Elizabeth smiled.

ALSO BY AMANDA MCCABE

The Elizabethan Mysteries

Murder at Hatfield Households

Murder at Westminster Abbey

Murder in the Queen's Garden

Murder at Whitehall

Murder at Fontainebleau

Murder at the Queen's Masquerade

The Santa Fe Revival 1920s Mysteries (as Amanda Allen)

Santa Fe Mourning

As Amanda McCabe

The Queen's Christmas Summons Tarnished Rose of the Court Lady Midnight

The Demure Miss Manning The Wallflower's Mistletoe Wedding

The Runaway Countess Running From Scandal

Secrets of a Wallflower: Debutantes in Paris Sea of Darkness: World of Gothic

ABOUT THE AUTHOR

Amanda Carmack is a pseudonym for for a multi-published author. Her books have been nominated for many awards, including the RITA Award, the Romantic Times Reviewer's Choice Award, the National Readers' Choice Award, and the HOLT Medallion. She lives in Santa Fe with a handsome husband, a bossy Poodle, and a lazy cat, and far too many books about the Tudors. You can visit her anytime at http://amandacarmack.com

www.ingramcontent.com/pod-product-compliance
Lightning Source LLC
Chambersburg PA
CBHW011516100726
47899CB00010BD/3384

* 9 7 8 1 6 4 8 3 9 2 6 8 9 *